The driver's door opened and her heart seemed to stall in her chest when Sheriff Patrick Martinez stepped out.

Broad shoulders, a tall, lean body gloved in jeans, a cowboy hat on his head. She tried to ignore her reaction to him, but it was as impossible as it had always been.

He strode toward her and Bree snapped out of the ridiculous trance she'd slipped into. Focus. She was a professional; he was a professional. There was no need to let personal feelings get in the way of doing the job.

"Sheriff," she said, taking the first step toward acting normal.

Vivid blue eyes zeroed in on Bree like a laser hitting its target. "Detective."

Together they investigated the crime scene, looking for clues, waiting for a story to unfold that would provide some answers.

In the meantime, Bree tried hard not to stare at Patrick's profile. This wasn't the time. No time would be right…not for the two of them.

Besides, being so near Patrick after all this time made her even more aware of how very much her son looked like him….

25 years of INTRIGUE®

Dear Harlequin Intrigue Reader,

In honor of two very special events, the Harlequin Intrigue editorial team has planned exceptional promotions to celebrate throughout 2009. To kick off the year, we're celebrating Harlequin Books' 60th Diamond Anniversary with DIAMONDS AND DADDIES, an exciting four-book miniseries featuring protective dads and their extraordinary proposals to four very lucky women. Rita Herron launches the series with *Platinum Cowboy* next month.

Later in the year Harlequin Intrigue celebrates its own 25th anniversary. To mark the event we've asked reader favorites to return with their most popular series.

• Debra Webb has created a new COLBY AGENCY trilogy. This time out, Victoria Colby-Camp will need to enlist the help of her entire staff of agents for her own family crisis.

• You can return to 43 LIGHT STREET with Rebecca York and join Caroline Burnes on another crime-solving mission with Familiar the Black Cat Detective.

• Next stop: WHITEHORSE, MONTANA with B.J. Daniels for more Big Sky mysteries with a new family. Meet the Corbetts—Shane, Jud, Dalton, Lantry and Russell.

Because we know our readers love following trace evidence, we've created the new continuity KENNER COUNTY CRIME UNIT. Whether collecting evidence or tracking down leads, lawmen and investigators have more than their jobs on the line, because the real mystery is one of the heart. Pick up *Secrets in Four Corners* by Debra Webb this month, and don't miss any one of the terrific stories to follow in this series.

And that's just a small selection of what we have planned to thank our readers.

We'd love to hear from you, and hope you enjoy all of our special promotions this year.

Happy reading, and happy anniversary, Harlequin Books!

Sincerely,

Denise Zaza
Senior Editor
Harlequin Intrigue

DEBRA WEBB

SECRETS IN FOUR CORNERS

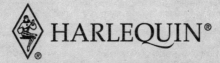

TORONTO • NEW YORK • LONDON
AMSTERDAM • PARIS • SYDNEY • HAMBURG
STOCKHOLM • ATHENS • TOKYO • MILAN • MADRID
PRAGUE • WARSAW • BUDAPEST • AUCKLAND

Colorado is a beautiful place. I've been blessed enough to spend time there and I was awed by the natural wonders. Please be advised that Kenner County is a fictional place, although many real towns and areas of interest were used in the creation of this story. As hard as an author works to do all the research necessary, there are times when a little something needs to be added in the best interest of the story. So if you find something missing or where it shouldn't be, please forgive me, and please, please enjoy Bree and Patrick's story!

Special thanks and acknowledgment to Debra Webb for her contribution to the Kenner County Crime Unit miniseries.

ISBN-13: 978-0-373-88882-5
ISBN-10:   0-373-88882-1

SECRETS IN FOUR CORNERS

Recycling programs
for this product may
not exist in your area.

www.eHarlequin.com

Printed in U.S.A.

ABOUT THE AUTHOR

Debra Webb was born in Scottsboro, Alabama, to parents who taught her that anything is possible if you want it bad enough. She began writing at age nine. Eventually, she met and married the man of her dreams, and tried some other occupations, including selling vacuum cleaners, working in a factory, a daycare center, a hospital and a department store. When her husband joined the military, they moved to Berlin, Germany, and Debra became a secretary in the commanding general's office. By 1985 they were back in the States, and finally moved to Tennessee, to a small town where everyone knows everyone else. With the support of her husband and two beautiful daughters, Debra took up writing again, looking to mysteries and movies for inspiration. In 1998, her dream of writing for Harlequin Books came true. You can write to Debra with your comments at P.O. Box 64, Huntland, Tennessee 37345, or visit her Web site at www.debrawebb.com to find out exciting news about her next book.

Books by Debra Webb

HARLEQUIN INTRIGUE

*Colby Agency
**The Specialists

CAST OF CHARACTERS

Detective Sabrina "Bree" Hunter—Bree represents the law and her people. But she has a secret that could destroy all that she is.

Sheriff Patrick Martinez—Patrick should never have let Bree walk away eight years ago. Working with her again drives that point home, but it's way too late for them.

Burt Hayes—Ute Tribal Park guide who discovers the body. Does he know more than he's telling?

Officer Steve Cyrus—Is he cut out to be a cop? He loses his lunch every time he discovers a body.

Callie MacBride—Head forensic scientist at the Kenner County Crime Lab. Something about this latest case is eating at her.

Special Agent in Charge Jerry Ortiz—Stationed at the Durango, Colorado, field office, Ortiz will seemingly stop at nothing to get to the bottom of who killed Agent Julie Grainger.

Special Agents Tom Ryan and Dylan Acevedo—They've come from far and wide to see that their friend's killer is brought to justice. But is her killer one of their own?

Sherman Watts—A lowlife weasel who just might be capable of anything.

Julie Grainger—A devoted special agent whose dead body is found. Can her death lead her friends and colleagues to the truth?

Vincent Del Gardo—Everything keeps pointing to him as the doer of the dirtiest of deeds.

Chapter One

Sabrina Hunter fastened her utility belt around her hips. "Eat up, Peter, or we're gonna be late."

Peter Hunter peered up at his mom, a spoonful of Cheerios halfway to his mouth. "We're always late."

This was definitely nothing to brag about. "But," his mother reminded him, "our New Year's resolution was to make it a point *not* to be late anymore." It was only January twelfth. Surely, they weren't going to break their resolution already.

Chewing his cereal thoughtfully, Peter tilted his dark head and studied her again. "Truth or dare?"

Bree took a deep breath, reached for

patience. "Eat. There's no time for games." She tucked her cell phone into her belt. Mondays were always difficult. Especially when Bree had worked the weekend and her son had spent most of that time with his aunt Tabitha. She spoiled the boy outrageously, as did her teenage daughter, Layla. Even so, Bree was glad to have her family support system when duty called, as it had this weekend. She grabbed her mug and downed the last of the coffee that had grown cold during her rush to prepare for the day.

Peter swallowed, then insisted, "Truth. Is my real daddy a jerk just like Big Jack?"

Bree choked. Coughed. She plopped her mug on the counter and stared at her son. "Where did you hear something like that?"

"Cousin Layla said so." He nodded resolutely. "Aunt Tabitha told her to hush 'cause I might hear. Is it true? Is my real daddy a jerk?"

"You must've misunderstood, Peter." *Breathe.* Bree moistened her lips and mentally scrambled for a way to change the subject. "Grab your coat and let's get you to school." Memories tumbled one over the other in her head. Memories she had sworn she would never allow back into her thoughts. That was her other New Year's resolution. After eight years it was past time she'd put *him* out of her head and her heart once and for all.

What the hell was her niece thinking, bringing *him* up? Particularly with Peter anywhere in the vicinity. The kid loved playing hide and seek, loved sneaking up on his mother and aunt even more. His curious nature ensured he missed very little. Tabitha and Layla knew this!

Bree ordered herself to calm down.

"Nope. I didn't misunderstand." Peter pushed back his chair, carefully picked up his cereal bowl and headed for the sink. He rinsed the bowl and placed it just as carefully into the dishwasher. "I heard her."

Bree's pulse rate increased. "Layla was probably talking about…" Bree racked her brain for a name, someone they all knew—anyone besides *him*.

Before she could come up with a name or a logical explanation for her niece's slip, Peter turned to his mother once more, his big blue eyes—the ones so much like his father's and so unlike her brown ones—resolute. "Layla said my real daddy—"

"Okay, okay." Bree held up her hands. "I got that part." How on earth was she supposed to respond? "We can talk on the way to school." Maybe that would at least buy her some time. And if she were really lucky Peter would get distracted and forget all about the subject of his father.

Something Bree herself would very much like to do.

She would be having a serious talk with her sister and niece.

Thankfully her son didn't argue. He tugged on his coat and picked up his backpack. So far, so good. She might just get out of this one after all. Was that selfish of her? Was Peter the one being cheated by her decision to keep the past in the past? Including his father?

Bree pushed the questions aside and

shouldered into the navy uniform jacket
that sported the logo of the Towaoc Police
Department. At the coat closet near her
front door, she removed the lockbox from
the top shelf, retrieved her service weapon
and holstered it. After high school she'd
gotten her associate's degree in criminal
justice. She hadn't looked back since,
spending a decade working in reservation
law enforcement. The invitation to join the
special homicide task force formed by the
Bureau of Indian Affairs and the Ute
Mountain Reservation tribal officials had
been exactly the opportunity she had been
looking for to further her career.

Besides her son and family, her career
was primary in her life. Not merely
because she was a single parent, either,
although that was a compelling enough
motive. She wanted to be a part of
changing the reservation's unofficial reputation as the murder capital of Colorado.
This was her home. Making a difference
was important to her. She wanted to do her
part for her people.

Not to mention work kept her busy. Kept her head on straight and out of that past she did not want to think about, much less talk about. An idle mind was like idle hands, it got one into trouble more often than not.

Enough trouble had come Bree's way the last few years.

No sooner had she slid behind the wheel of her SUV and closed the door had Peter demanded, "Truth, Mommy." He snapped his safety belt into place.

So much for any hopes of him letting the subject go. Bree glanced over her shoulder to the backseat where her son waited. She could take the easy way out and say his aunt and cousin were right. His curiosity would be satisfied and that would be the end of that—for now anyway. But that would be a lie. There were a lot of things she could say about the man who'd fathered her child, but that he was bad or the kind of jerk her ex, Jack, had turned out to be definitely wasn't one of them.

"Your father was never anything like

Big Jack." Even as she said the words, her heart stumbled traitorously.

"So he was a good guy?"

Another question that required a cautiously worded response. "A really good guy."

"Like a superhero?"

Maybe that was a stretch. But her son was into comics lately. "I guess you could say that." Guilt pricked her again for allowing the conversation to remain in past tense…as if his father were deceased. Another selfish gesture on her part.

But life was so much easier that way.

"Am I named after him?"

Tension whipped through Bree. That was a place she definitely didn't want to go. Her cell phone vibrated. Relief flared. Talk about being saved by the bell, or, in this case, the vibration. "Hold on, honey." Bree withdrew the phone from the case on her belt and opened it. "Hunter."

"Detective Hunter, this is Officer Danny Brewer."

Though she was acquainted with a fair

number of local law enforcement members, particularly those on the reservation, the name didn't strike a chord. She couldn't readily associate the name with one department or the other, making it hard to anticipate whether his call was something or nothing. That didn't prevent a new kind of tension from sending her instincts to the next level. "What can I do for you, Officer Brewer?"

"Well, ma'am, we have a situation."

His tone told her far more than his words. *Something*.

When she would have asked for an explanation, he went on, "We have a one eighty-seven."

Adrenaline fired in Bree's veins. Before she could launch the barrage of homicide-related questions that instantly sprang to mind, Brewer tacked on, "My partner said I should call you. He would've called himself but he's been busy puking his guts out ever since we took a look at the...vic."

Damn. Another victim.

Bree blinked, focused on the details she knew so far. Puking? Had to be Officer Steve Cyrus. She knew him well. Poor Cyrus lost his last meal at every scene involving a body.

One eighty-seven.

Damn.

Another murder.

"Location?" Bree glanced at her son. She would drop him off at school and head straight to the scene. Hell of a way to start a Monday morning. Frustration hit on the heels of the adrenaline. She'd worked a case of rape and attempted murder just this weekend. As hard as her team toiled to prevent as well as solve violent crimes it never seemed to be enough.

"The Tribal Park." Brewer cleared his throat. "In the canyon close to the Two-Story House. One of the guides who checks the trails a couple of times a week during the off-season found the victim."

"Don't let him out of your sight," Bree reminded. She would need to question the guide at length. Chances were he would be the closest thing to a witness, albeit after the fact, she would get. "Did you ID the victim?" She hoped this wasn't another rape as well. Twelve days into the New Year and they'd had two of those already. Both related to drug use.

Bree frowned at the muffled conversation taking place on the other end of the line. It sounded like Brewer was asking his partner what he should say in answer to her question. Weird.

"Ma'am," Brewer said, something different in his voice now, "Steve said just get here as fast as you can. He'll explain the details then."

When the call ended Bree stared at her phone then shook her head.

Damned weird.

"M-o-o-o-m," Peter said, drawing out the single syllable, "you didn't answer my question."

She definitely didn't have time for that now. More of that guilt heaped on her shoulders at just how relieved she was to have an excuse not to go there. "We'll have to talk about it later. That was another police officer who called. I have to get to work."

Peter groaned, but didn't argue with her. He knew that for his mom work meant something bad had happened to someone.

As Bree guided her vehicle into the school's drop-off lane, she considered her little boy. She wanted life on the reservation to continue to improve. For him. For the next generation, period. As hard as she worked, at times it never seemed to be enough.

"Have a good day, sweetie." She smoothed his hair and kissed the top of his head.

His cheeks instantly reddened. "Mom."

Bree smiled as he hopped out of the SUV and headed for Towaoc Elementary's front entrance. Her baby was growing up. Her smile faded. There would be more questions about his father.

She couldn't think about that right now.

Right now she had a homicide to investigate.

ONLY A FEW minutes on Highway 160 were required to reach the Ute Mountain Tribal Park. She turned into the park entrance near the visitor's center, a former gas station that had been repurposed. Getting into the park was easy, reaching the ancient cliff face Ancestral Puebloan dwellings was another story.

A rough dirt road barely wide enough for her SUV was the only way besides making the trek on foot or horseback. The SUV bumped over the rutted dirt road. Twice Bree was forced to maneuver around ottoman-sized boulders from a recent rock slide. The road, which was more of a trail, was definitely better suited for traveling by horse or on foot. Since time was of the essence she would just have to deal with the less than favorable driving conditions. Every minute wasted allowed the possibility of trace evidence contamination or loss of that essential evidence entirely.

The harsh, barren landscape had a character wholly of its own. Basins with scatterings of sage and juniper and pine forests broke up the thousands of acres of desolation. Gray cliffs and brick-red buttes soaked up the scorching sun that even in the dead of winter and cloaked with snow somehow kept the temps comfortable enough most of the time. Not much otherwise in the way of color, but the amazing Colorado sky made up for it with vivid shades of blue broken only by the snow-capped peaks that added another layer of enchantment.

In the distance, providing a dramatic backdrop, was the giant Sleeping Ute Mountain. The name had come from the fact that the mountain's shape gave the appearance of a giant warrior sleeping on his back with arms crossed over his chest. The stories about the cliff dwellings and the great sleeping warrior who'd become a mountain had kept her enthralled as a kid.

At close to fifty degrees, it could have been a nice day. Bree sighed as she caught sight of the official Ute Reservation police SUV. A beat-up old pickup, probably belonging to the guide, was parked next to the SUV.

Another murder.

The idea that Steve Cyrus wanted her on the scene before he passed along any known details nagged at her again. What was with the mystery?

She parked her vehicle, grabbed a pair of latex gloves from her console and climbed out. She headed toward the cliffs where the two-story, sandstone dwelling hung, a proud, crumbling reminder of the residents who built them more than a millennium ago. The dwellings here were every bit as breathtaking as Mesa Verde's, but this park didn't get near the tourist flow. Primarily because no one came in without an official Ute guide. Preservation was far too important to her people.

Both officers as well as the guide waited some fifty yards from the area where during tourist season folks scrambled up the cliff face to check out the condos of the past. The perpetrator apparently hadn't been too concerned with concealing the body, though the location was definitely off the beaten path to some degree, particularly this time of year. Yet, most anyone who might have been out here could have stumbled over the scene. Or the act in progress.

Just another strange element.

As if her instincts had picked up on something in the air, her pulse rate quickened.

"Hunter," Steve Cyrus called out as he headed in her direction. "I need a minute." He hustled over to meet her.

"What's going on?" She glanced to where Brewer and the old man waited. "You got a body or what?"

Cyrus sent an oddly covert glance in that same direction. "Before you take a look there's something you need to know."

This got stranger by the moment. Bree held up her hands. "Wait—have you called the lab? The coroner?" The realization that no one—*no one*—else had arrived as of yet abruptly cut through all the confusion.

Cyrus shook his head, looked at the ground before meeting her gaze. "To tell you the truth, I didn't know who the hell to call first. This is…complicated. That's why I called you before anyone else."

"What the hell are you talking about, Cyrus?" Good grief, it wasn't like this was the first deceased victim he'd come upon.

"The vic…" He scrubbed a hand over his chin. "She's…"

At least Bree now knew that the victim was female.

"She's a federal agent."

Federal agent? "BIA?" Her first thought was that an agent from the Bureau of Indian Affairs had been murdered. The controversy over who was boss, Tribal Affairs or BIA, was an ongoing issue. Things got complicated and damned hot at times.

Cyrus shook his head. "FBI. Julie Grainger."

Regret hardened to a lump in Bree's gut. She'd only met Julie Grainger once. Nice lady. Young, early thirties, like Bree. Hard worker. Loyal. A damned good agent from all indications.

"I told you this was complicated."

No kidding. "All right." Bree rubbed

her forehead, an ache starting there. "I'll take a look and talk to the guide. You call Callie MacBride and get her lab techs over here. Tell her it's Grainger." A mixture of frustration and more of that regret dragged at Bree's shoulders. "Then call the coroner's office." *Think, Bree. This one will be sticky. Protocol has to be followed to the letter.*

"You want me to call Sheriff Martinez?" Cyrus suggested.

A vise clamped around Bree's chest. This was Kenner County…of course the sheriff would need to be involved. Bree heard herself say yes. What else could she say? Then she did an about-face, her movements stiff, and headed to where Brewer and the guide waited.

Patrick Martinez.

No matter that he had been the sheriff of the county for the last six years, somehow she had managed to avoid running into him. They hadn't spoken in nearly eight years.

Eight years!

Focus on the job.

Special Agent Julie Grainger was dead. She deserved Bree's full attention.

Nothing else mattered right now. Determining why she was dead and who killed her was top priority. "Yeah, do that. But call the others first."

"Morning, Detective," Brewer said as she approached.

"Good morning, Officer Brewer."

"This is Burt Hayes." Brewer gestured to the guide.

Hayes was Ute, as all park guides were. Bree's family was Ute, as well. Hayes had that aged, craggy look, the one that said he'd spent almost as much time in the scorching Western sun as the Puebloan dwellings. He wore faded jeans and beneath the matching denim jacket an equally faded khaki shirt, along with leather boots that had seen far better days. His graying hair was pulled into a ponytail that reached the middle of his back.

"Mr. Hayes." Bree extended her hand, gave his a firm shake. "I need to take a look around, then I'd like to ask you a few questions."

Hayes nodded. "You Charlie Hunter's girl?"

Most folks around the Four Corners area knew her father. He'd once been an outspoken advocate for the Ute people and tribal affairs…before a stroke had silenced his deep, strong voice.

"Yes, sir." Bree smiled. "And he's still as ornery as ever." She turned to Officer Brewer. "Why don't you assist Mr. Hayes with filling out his statement while I have a look at the scene?"

Brewer nodded, didn't comment or ask any questions, which meant that neither he nor Cyrus had done that part yet. Learning the victim was a federal agent had shaken them both.

Complicated.

Definitely complicated.

The silence felt deafening as Bree tugged on the latex gloves and crouched next to the victim nestled amid the rocks ensconced in the desert sand. Grainger's slender body was bloated with the ugliness of death, her skin pale and marbleized. One hand had been ravaged by wildlife, probably coyotes. Bree grimaced. They were damned lucky there wasn't more damage.

Bree visually examined the body for indications of the kind of violence done by man. No blood. Redness and bruising on the throat. No other signs of violence were visible except ligature marks on her throat. Bree leaned as close as possible and studied the marks. A unique pattern…not mere twine, certainly not a particularly thin wire. The longer she looked the more familiar the pattern appeared. Maybe a necklace of some sort. She'd definitely seen something like it before. Though Bree felt fairly certain cause of death was strangulation, the coroner would make the final conclusion.

She sat back on her haunches and inventoried more details. Jeans, blouse, which, on closer inspection, had a tear in one sleeve as if she'd struggled briefly with her attacker. Hiking boots. But no jacket.

Though the weather was definitely tolerable, the last couple of days the temps had hovered in the lower forties. Jacket wearing weather for sure.

Bree surveyed the landscape. No vehicle. She wandered wide around the body, careful of every step. No visible shoe imprints. With the dusty terrain and the ever-present wind, that was no real surprise. No purse. No cell phone. Most females carried some sort of purse, even if only a small clutch. And cell phones, hardly anyone left home without them these days.

Had the body been dumped here, making this location the secondary crime scene, or had Grainger met someone here who had taken her personal effects and vehicle after taking her life?

This part of the park's entry and exit possibilities via vehicle were limited to say the least.

The thought drew Bree's gaze to the road. A dust cloud bloomed, announcing that someone was coming…fast. An SUV bucked along the trail-turned-road until it skidded to a halt next to Bree's vehicle. The dust settled and her denial-swaddled brain registered what her eyes had already recognized.

Official vehicle.

Kenner County.

Had Cyrus called the sheriff first? Now that she thought about it, that didn't add up. There was no way the sheriff could have gotten here this fast unless he'd heard already. Before Cyrus called anyone.

The driver's-side door opened and her heart seemed to stall in her chest. A booted foot hit the ground as the trademark white cowboy hat rose above the open door. Broad shoulders followed that same route…then a tall, lean body gloved in jeans and a brown sheriff's department jacket moved aside and the driver's-side door slammed shut.

Patrick Martinez.

Sheriff Patrick Martinez.

Peter's father.

He strode toward her and Bree snapped

out of the ridiculous trance she'd slipped into. Focus. She was a professional; he was a professional. There was no need to let personal feelings get in the way of doing the job. She'd considered long and hard what she would do if this situation ever arose. Now was the time to put that plan into action.

"Sheriff," she said, taking the first step.

Vivid blue eyes, ones exactly like her son's, zeroed in on Bree's like a laser hitting its target. Patrick nodded curtly. "Detective."

"The victim's over here." Bree walked back to where Grainger's body lay waiting to reveal the story behind the final moments of her life.

Had Cyrus or Brewer called MacBride yet? Those lab folks should be here. Now.

Patrick crouched to get a closer look. Bree did the same. He pulled a pair of latex gloves from his jacket pocket and tugged them on. "Who found her?"

The pain in his deep voice reflected the ache of finding one of his own murdered.

Every victim was a tragedy, but the loss of a colleague was like losing a family member.

"Burt Hayes. Park guide." Hayes was still giving his statement to Brewer. "He checks the trails every couple of days. Found her this morning. Looks like she may have been here a couple of days."

Patrick nodded. Bree tried hard not to stare at his profile. This wasn't the time. No time would be right…not for the two of them. Still, she couldn't look away. Strong, square jaw. He hadn't taken the time to shave that morning, but the stubble looked good on him. Always had. For a man closer to forty than thirty, he looked damned good.

Being so near Patrick after all this time made her even more aware of how very much her son looked like him.

"Coroner on his way?"

Bree blinked. Concentrate. "Officer Cyrus called the coroner and Callie MacBride at the crime lab just before you arrived."

"But he didn't call me." Patrick rose, towered over her before her brain could send the message to her suddenly rubbery legs to stand. He took a long look around the area. "You and your people sure got out here in one hell of a hurry."

The accusation in the sheriff's eyes when his gaze settled on hers once more ticked her off, exiled all the other emotional confusion of seeing him again after eight years…after the discussion with her son not an hour ago…after everything.

"Cyrus was about to call your office when you arrived." She lifted her chin, sent a lead-filled gaze right back at him. "The initial call came into TPD, Cyrus and Brewer got here first, then called me. Obviously someone called you."

"We got a 9-1-1 call," he explained. "The caller didn't identify himself, but there was no question that he was male." Patrick jerked his head toward the guide. "Any idea why he would call your department and report his discovery, then call 9-1-1?"

Bree glanced at the old man. Most of the older folks didn't bother will cell phones.

Many didn't even have landlines. Chances were he'd gone to the gas station on Highway 160 and made the call from there since the visitor's center wouldn't have been open so early. But why call twice? She shook her head. That was something she needed to ask him.

Should have already, but she'd only been on the scene a few minutes herself. Still, she felt stupid at the moment. Patrick Martinez somehow always made her feel inept. That had been part of their problem. Here she'd been all caught up in the emotional impact of seeing him again. And he was only concerned with why he didn't get the call first. Not to mention they should both be focused on the investigation, not some petty pissing contest.

Okay, that wasn't exactly true. His point was relevant. Whatever the case, it was past time to cut to the chase here. "As I said, Officers Cyrus and Brewer were the first on the scene. Cyrus called me immediately due to the sensitivity of the situation. We work together. It made sense at the time. It wasn't about leaving you or anyone else out. As for the 9-1-1 call, we'll have to ask Mr. Hayes." She folded her arms over her chest, refused to waver beneath his iron stare. "Bottom line, this is Ute territory first and foremost. Cyrus's decision to call me first was the right one."

The stare-off lasted another eight or ten seconds before Patrick looked away. Bree did a little mental victory dance. It hadn't been her to give this time.

"I'll call my Bureau contact." Patrick shook his head, rested his gaze on hers once more. "There's going to be a firestorm over this," he warned. "There won't be any straightforward lines of jurisdiction beyond the fact that the Bureau will be lead. We'll do what they tell us. But everyone will want a part of this. Unfortunately that includes every damned news network in this part of the country."

He spoke as if she were a rookie straight out of the academy. "Was that announcement for your benefit? 'Cause I sure as hell hope it wasn't for mine. I know how the chain of command works, Martinez. And I also know the full scope of the kind of impact this case will have on the community. I don't need you or anyone else to tell me how to do my job."

With one long, slow sweep of his dark lashes, he looked her up and down. "If working together is going to be a problem for you, perhaps you should step aside and let one of the other detectives on the special task force take this one."

He had to be kidding. Was he trying to piss her off? Fury boiled up inside her. "I don't have a problem. You're the one who appears to have a problem. You rode in here with a chip on your shoulder. I came to do my job. Why don't *you* step aside and assign one of your deputies to this investigation? That way we'll both be happy."

Another ten seconds of dramatic silence elapsed with the two of them staring holes through each other.

"I can leave the past where it belongs," he offered, his tone a little less accusatory but no less bitter.

Enough with this game. "What past?" With that she gave him her back and stalked off to do her job.

This was murder. The murder of a federal agent. It was way bigger than their foolish past.

Time to do more than just talk about it.

Chapter Two

She hadn't changed a bit.

Patrick watched Bree walk away.

Long dark hair always kept in a braid. As a detective she wasn't required to wear the blue uniform, but she did as a matter of pride. She represented her people as well as the police department.

For nearly eight years he had staunchly avoided running into her. Even after the powers that be in Kenner County had persuaded him to come to Colorado and serve as sheriff, in the jurisdiction where she lived, he'd managed to get by without contact. He'd heard that since they'd parted ways she had married a Ute man. It had been fairly easy to pretend he didn't care.

Now here they were…working a case together. And neither one of them was willing to back off.

His gaze settled on the place where the victim lay amid the rocks and dirt of the barren landscape. A scrap of desert grass managed to thrive here and there around her position. Bleak was the word that came to mind…both for the place and the victim.

Julie Grainger.

Patrick hadn't known the agent other than in passing. He'd met her once at a briefing. Professional, compassionate and dedicated.

Now she was dead.

Patrick shook his head. An incredible waste.

Unable to delay the inevitable any longer, he put through a call to Special Agent in Charge Jerry Ortiz of the Federal Bureau of Investigation Durango field office that represented the Four Corners area. Making this kind of call to someone who no doubt knew the victim well was Patrick's least favorite duty.

But someone had to do it.

Ortiz wasn't in the office so Patrick was patched through to his cell phone. Ortiz had already heard the news from Callie MacBride. He was shocked and devastated. He'd called his people to set things in motion. His staff, those who knew Grainger as well as those who didn't, would be stunned as well.

Patrick ended the call, a sickening feeling in the pit of his gut. A damned shame.

He turned all the way around and surveyed the barren land once more. What the hell had Grainger been doing out here? He was certain a highly trained agent wouldn't have met an informant, much less a suspect, in such a secluded setting. Not without compelling motivation. His initial conclusion was that this had to be the secondary crime scene. Meaning she'd been dumped here like a piece of trash.

Fury thundered inside him. As much as he loved the Four Corners area—it was his home—he hated the scum that had recently flocked here. Worse, he despised the lowlifes who were born and bred here. It seemed the harder he worked to clean up the county where he'd been raised, the harder evil worked to worm its way into his territory.

He couldn't stop the spread of drugs and crime; he was, after all, only one man. But he could damned sure do all within his power to slow it down.

Officers Brewer and Cyrus were busy securing the scene, which should have been done immediately upon discovery. Patrick could only assume that the officers had been too overwhelmed by the discovery that the victim was a federal agent to act judiciously. He moved cautiously around the perimeter of the zone now officially designated by yellow tape as the crime scene. No tire tracks other than those of the vehicles parked nearby. No shoe imprints besides the ones belonging to those currently on the scene. The folks from the crime lab would sweep the area for evidence but so far he saw nothing but an abandoned soda can and a cigarette pack wrapper. Both of which would be analyzed just in case.

A cloud of dust announced the arrival of more official vehicles. The crime lab folks, he hoped. The sooner the scene was searched for clues the greater the likelihood that any evidence left behind would be found.

Patrick met the SUV as it skidded to a stop. All four doors opened. Callie MacBride, head forensic scientist at the Kenner County Crime Unit, climbed out of the front passenger-side door. Her face was pale, strained with disbelief and regret.

"Callie, this is a damned shame." Patrick exhaled a heavy breath. There wasn't a hell of a lot more to say. Not at this point. He had no idea what case Grainger had been working any more than he knew any personal contacts that might have brought her to this place.

Callie dipped her head in acknowledgment of his inadequate words. "Patrick, I believe you know most of my team." She indicated her associates who had emerged from the vehicle. "Miguel Acevedo, Bart Fleming and Bobby O'Shea."

Patrick shook the hand of each man in turn and offered his sincere condolences. He'd worked with about every member of the crime unit the past couple of years. The Four Corners area had needed a crime lab for a good long while before the powers that be finally had the sense to make it a reality. Times like this were the reason. Every single member of the team had made Kenner County home; they knew the land and its people. In the past, law enforcement had had to rely on state facilities from as far away as Denver.

These folks would get the job done quickly and thoroughly with the kind of knowledge only gained through life experience with the people and the land. That the victim was one of their own made their work this morning more than a job.

This was personal.

Faces grim, the team gathered their gear and donned protective wear. There would be little Patrick could do until their work was finished. The crime lab unit was made up of a number of other highly trained personnel. Though Patrick had worked with each of them at one time or another, he dealt primary with Callie on the vast majority of cases.

As personal as this case was, Patrick didn't worry about those personal feelings getting in the way. The Kenner County Crime Unit was small in size and funds were limited for equipment, but the scientists and technicians were top-notch. The best of the best. Particularly Callie.

Patrick stayed out of the way and let them do their job. The extended moment of silence as the group acknowledged their fallen colleague was painful to watch. Callie MacBride in particular appeared shaken to the very core. Patrick wondered if she'd known the victim personally as well as professionally. That possibility was very likely, considering the whole staff operated as much as a family as a team of colleagues.

While Callie's people did their work,

Patrick turned his attention to the Ute guide who had discovered the body. He doubted the man had seen anything but there were questions that needed to be asked. Like why he'd called the Towaoc police and then put in an anonymous call to 9-1-1, evidently some minutes later.

With that in mind, Patrick started in his direction. Bree was interviewing the guide and would no doubt ask those same questions, but it was Patrick's job to ensure every base was covered. Officers Cyrus and Brewer were maintaining the perimeter. If word got out that a federal agent had been murdered the media would flock to the park like vultures ready to pick the kill.

Damn. The reality of what they were doing here hit Patrick all over again.

A federal agent was dead.

Murder was murder and any loss was one too many, but this loss took the act to a higher level. That Grainger, like all in law enforcement, served this community made the business of murder even uglier.

Bree turned to face Patrick as he neared.

Judging by her expression there was trouble with the guide's story. "Mr. Hayes only made one call," she said. "That call was to the Towaoc Police Department. Your 9-1-1 caller was not Mr. Hayes."

Patrick's senses moved to a higher state of alert. That meant two things right out of the gate. The recorded 9-1-1 call could very well turn out to be their only tangible evidence. And the caller might just be the killer.

"Mr. Hayes," Patrick addressed the older man, working to keep his composure free of the frustration and impatience despite the anticipation zinging through him. "I'm certain Detective Hunter has already asked, but I need you to think long and hard about the questions I'm going to ask before you answer."

The man nodded, glanced briefly at Bree.

Patrick understood that Hayes was anxious as well. This wasn't a situation anyone wanted to be caught in. Finding a dead Caucasian female on reservation territory was about the last thing a Ute man would want on his plate. The political climate wasn't that different from a few decades ago when Patrick had been in school and distinct cultural lines had been drawn. The undercurrent of racial differences remained a nagging social challenge that played itself out within the criminal element of the area.

"What time did you arrive at the park this morning?"

Hayes looked from Patrick to Bree. He'd already answered this question. Patrick understood that, but he needed the man to think…to be absolutely certain of his answers and to give them again. And maybe again after that. Before this case was solved, Hayes would likely be questioned several times. Patrick and Bree could compare his responses later and analyze any possible discrepancies or suggestions of deception.

Hayes scratched his head. "Before seven o'clock. I stop at Rudy's each morning. Six a.m. From there I come here."

"Rudy's is the service station back at the turnoff to the park entrance," Bree explained.

Patrick knew the place. "Was there a

reason you came to this particular place first?" The park was a big place. Patrick needed to know if Hayes had a routine for checking the area.

"I check the dwellings first. This one." He indicated the two-story dwelling. "Then the next. Lately there's been trouble with teenagers using them as hangouts. So I check them first."

"Did you meet anyone as you entered the park this morning? Anything you might have seen could be important," Patrick emphasized. He watched the man's eyes and facial expressions closely. "No matter how unimportant it may seem, there may be something we can learn from the slightest detail. A vehicle parked nearby on the main highway. Anything."

Hayes contemplated the question half a minute before shaking his head. "No one was here except her." He gestured to where the lab folks were methodically working the scene. "It was quiet. Nobody around. Just the dead woman."

"Mr. Hayes," Bree interjected, "believes

he returned to Rudy's shortly after seven and made the call to TPD, then he came straight back here and waited for the police to arrive."

That meant the other caller had been here and gone before that since Hayes hadn't encountered anyone and yet the unknown caller hadn't reached out to 9-1-1 immediately. His call hadn't come in until a quarter past eight.

Anytime someone discovered a body and didn't call it in immediately, he was either puking, crying, or he was afraid. Dispatch had indicated the caller sounded male and had no particular accent. Hayes didn't have an accent per se but his speech pattern was somewhat slow, his words not necessarily the first choice to use by those educated in public schools.

Drawing further suspicion, when asked to identify himself the 9-1-1 caller had ended the call—which almost certainly meant he had something to hide. Whether motivated by fear or guilt, the caller had to be found and questioned.

"You're certain you came straight back here," Patrick pressed. "You didn't talk to anyone at the store about what you'd found? Not even the owner? Is there any possibility that perhaps someone over-heard you?"

Hayes shook his head resolutely. "I didn't talk to anyone. I don't think anyone heard me. I came back here as fast as my old truck would carry me."

Patrick visually assessed the old truck. Not that fast, he imagined. "What time did you get your call?" he asked Bree.

She checked her cell. "Seven-fifty."

Hayes couldn't have missed the 9-1-1 caller by more than a few minutes.

"Thank you, Mr. Hayes." Patrick wanted to discuss this turn of events with Callie. "We will be in touch with additional questions. This is standard procedure."

Hayes grunted and gave Bree a nod. She thanked the man as well and Officer Cyrus escorted him to his truck to finish his written statement and to obtain pertinent information in terms of how to reach him.

"I know how to question a witness."

Patrick's attention snapped back to Bree. A frown pulled at his brow. "I'm well aware of your abilities as an investigator, Bree." Bree…he hadn't said her name out loud in a long, long time. His gut knotted even now as it echoed through him. He'd loved her….

But that was a long time ago.

Fury etched itself across the delicate lines of her face. A face he'd been hard-pressed to erase from his dreams most every night for nearly eight years now.

"There was no need to reask every single question I'd already posed to Mr. Hayes. What you did undermined my authority and my ability. I don't appreciate it one damned bit."

Patrick didn't have to remind her that he was the county sheriff and this was his jurisdiction the same as it was hers. Doing so would only anger her all the more. "You did your job and I did mine. Mr. Hayes will be asked those same questions and more by numerous others during the course of this investigation. I'm sure you understand how protocol works when jurisdiction crosses the usual boundaries."

Judging by the deeper shade of red that climbed up her neck and across her face, his explanation hadn't been what she'd wanted to hear. If she expected an apology, she could forget it.

"This conversation is pointless." She tugged at the lapels of her jacket. "Callie MacBride needs to know about this. The audio recording of the 9-1-1 call will need to be analyzed in a different light. I, for one, would like to hear it for myself."

He threw up his hands in surrender. "You took the words right out of my mouth."

Lips tight, eyes blazing, Bree executed an about-face and stalked off.

Patrick followed. All these years he'd told himself that if the situation arose he could work with Bree. At this point, there was no logical reason professionalism shouldn't override their personal history.

So much for logic.

Agent Acevedo snapped digital photographs of the scene and the victim. Patrick swallowed hard. Each time he considered Agent Grainger the victim, his gut tightened. Agents O'Shea and Fleming searched the zone within the cordoned-off area and tagged possible evidence. From what Patrick had noted there wasn't much but for now anything and everything had to be ruled out. A time-consuming process to say the least.

Bree approached Callie first. The two stepped aside and Patrick joined the huddle. Bree might not like the fact that he was on this case, but she would simply have to get over it.

Once the facts they had discovered regarding the two calls were passed along, Bree added, "I don't know what we'll learn from the audio recording, but it's worth a shot."

"Absolutely," Callie agreed.

"How soon can you arrange to have the recording at your lab?" Patrick glanced at his watch. "It's almost nine now. I can get the request started while you finish your work here."

When ten or so seconds passed with Callie seemingly lost in thought, he added, "I know the Bureau will be lead on this investigation, but whatever my department can do we're completely at your disposal."

"The same goes for my department," Bree assured her. "The task force is working a couple of other homicides, but I'm certain we can manage some additional personnel to support this investigation."

Patrick recognized that Bree was only doing her job. Still, it felt like they were in competition. That was one issue he had to get under control. Clear the air somehow. Evidently, eight years apart hadn't done the job.

"We'll be here," Callie finally said, her voice as well as her expression distracted, "for several hours." She rubbed her forehead, the gesture uncharacteristic for the hard-nosed, professional lady he knew. "Let's say three o'clock at the lab. I'll put in a call to Olivia. She can cut through the red tape faster than your office and have the recording available sooner." This she directed to Patrick.

"That'll work." Olivia Perez was a go-getter. Like the others on Callie's team, Olivia wouldn't rest until her task was accomplished.

"Meanwhile," Bree offered, "I can begin checking with nearby businesses, like Rudy's, and get a rundown of the customers who come through his station early each morning. Maybe I'll get lucky and find someone who saw something. The locals stay pretty aware of what's going on around them. Any strangers or unfamiliar faces will stick out in their minds. Most will talk to me."

When they might not talk to Patrick or his deputies. She didn't have to say that part. Patrick knew from experience. "I'll go along with you," he said to Bree. The way her eyes widened and her breath caught made him relatively certain she would rather swallow broken glass. "We'll get more done together."

She blinked. "Of course." She turned to Callie then. "I'll keep you posted if we learn anything before the meeting this afternoon."

Callie nodded vaguely, then rejoined her team. Patrick watched her unnatural movements. Stiff. Uncertain. Totally opposite the confident woman he'd seen in action many, many times. Something was troubling her. Something more than the fact that a colleague, and perhaps friend, was dead.

Right now all they had were questions. What had brought Agent Grainger to this desolate place in the dead of winter…all alone? Had she been tailing a suspect? Or meeting with an informant?

There were some signs of a struggle, but not enough to warrant the belief that Grainger had in fact fiercely attempted to defend herself. Whoever her attacker was, he'd moved swiftly and with his victim unaware.

For a skilled agent like Grainger, that was no easy task.

He dragged his thoughts back to the here

and now just in time to see Bree settle behind the wheel of her SUV and slam the door.

Damn. She wasn't going to make any part of this easy. He strode to her vehicle, opened the passenger-side door without waiting for an invitation and said, "I guess this means I'm riding with you."

She started the engine, didn't spare him a glance. "Suit yourself. I'm always happy to cooperate fully with the sheriff's department."

Not the slightest bit easy.

Going door-to-door might not garner any information, but right now it was their only option. Until they were briefed—if they were briefed—on Agent Grainger's activities just prior to her death, basic legwork was about the only hand they had to play. As the investigation moved into full swing, the Bureau would lay out the ground rules. Until then, they'd have to play this by the seat of their pants.

Patrick glanced at the driver. Maybe, if he were really, really lucky, he'd get through this without saying or doing anything he would regret the way he regretted so much else that had happened between them.

Like the past eight years.

Chapter Three

He was in her SUV.

Bree covertly scanned the interior of the vehicle. Had her son left anything lying around? A favorite toy or game? Were there indications she had a child? She didn't breathe easy until she felt satisfied that there was nothing for Patrick to notice.

"Where would you suggest we start?"

The deep sound of his voice resonating inside her vehicle almost made her jump. *Stay cool.* Patrick was far too good at picking up on tension. Especially hers. The last thing she needed was for him to start asking personal questions.

"Rudy's." Since the visitor's center wasn't open, Hayes had made his phone call to TPD from the service station just outside the park. Made sense to begin there. To trace his steps, so to speak.

That Patrick didn't argue told her he agreed. She would like to feel flattered that he concurred with her conclusion but the choice was elementary. It wasn't like they had that many.

Rudy's Stop and Go had been around for as long as Bree could remember. The one gas stop for a number of miles in either direction. Outside Rudy's there were a few tourist traps that wouldn't be open before ten. At this time of the morning an employee could be inside stocking shelves and preparing for the business day to begin, but there was little likelihood anyone would have seen the vehicles passing on the highway.

Basically what Bree and Patrick were doing now was going through the motions. Until they knew what cases Grainger may have been working on in the area, or who her enemies were suspected to be, there was no other starting place.

The most primitive of police work.

Bree parked in front of Rudy's and climbed out of her vehicle. She didn't wait for Patrick, the less eye contact and conversation the better. She didn't need him analyzing her every move. And he was a master at scrutinizing and forming conclusions based on nothing more than his suspects' body language.

She felt exactly like that…a suspect.

Perhaps guilt had something to do with her defensiveness.

Inside the store the woman behind the counter glanced up as the bell over the door jingled. Bree flashed the cashier a smile then turned to wait for Patrick, who still lingered in the parking lot. He had paused to survey the parking lot and highway beyond. He walked to the west end of the building and peered toward the turnoff to the Tribal Park. She remembered that he liked to get a feel for the vicinity where a crime had taken place. To form scenarios related to the crime. That obviously hadn't changed.

Frustrating the hell out of her was the fact that her gaze roamed the breadth of his shoulders and the height of his tall frame from the cowboy boots to the familiar hat before she could rein in the reaction to seeing him again. But what really burned her was the way her heart pounded a little harder just watching him move. How could the organ be so mutinous?

This moment had been inevitable. She had contemplated that realization many times. They worked in the same county. It had only been a matter of time before the two of them ended up on a case together.

And still she wasn't ready for this.

When he turned to enter the store, she shifted in the other direction and went in search of Rudy Johnson, the owner.

"Good morning, Mr. Johnson."

"Good morning to you, Detective Hunter." The spry old man hesitated in his inventory duties and shot her a wide smile.

"How's the family?" The instant the words left her lips she could have bitten off her tongue. The bell over the door jingled announcing Patrick's entrance. Rudy would no doubt return the social gesture and ask about her son. Damn! She had to get her act together. The line she walked was precarious enough without tipping the balance unnecessarily.

A wave of uncertainty washed over her. How could she possibly hope to keep this up? Was she making a mistake hiding the truth from Patrick? From Peter? She'd made that decision a long time ago. At a time when her emotions had been particularly raw and she had been terrified of the consequences of telling him he had a son.

Too late to turn back now.

"The wife's arthritis is acting up," Rudy said as he tucked the pencil behind his ear. "But that's to be expected at our age." The smile broadened to a grin and his eyes twinkled. "How's Peter? I still owe him that trip to the cabin."

Patrick came to a stop right beside Bree as if the gods had deemed her guilty as charged and opted to torture her a little as a sneak preview of what was to come. This time the pounding in her chest had nothing to do with his nearness. "He's doing great. We'll have to get together soon and schedule that trip to your cabin." *Change the subject!* "Unfortunately, I'm here this morning on police business. Sheriff Martinez and I need to ask you a few questions. It'll only take a couple minutes."

Rudy looked from Bree to Patrick and back. Don't say any more about Peter, she urged silently.

"This about Burt Hayes?" Rudy placed his clipboard atop a row of canned goods and gave Bree his full attention. "He rushed back in here this morning to use the phone. The man was acting a mite strange. I asked him if there was trouble but he rushed outta here like the devil himself was on his heels." Rudy raised a speculative eyebrow. "I figured there was trouble at one of the dwellings."

"Did Hayes mention any problem?" Patrick inquired before Bree could.

Rudy shook his head. "Just asked to use the phone. Lizzy was using the one at the counter so I let him use the phone in the office." He hitched his thumb toward the door in the back marked Employees Only. "We had a regular morning rush at the time, so I didn't get to ask him what the problem was."

"Before eight this morning did you notice anyone else behaving strangely?" Bree ventured, unsure just how much Patrick had in mind sharing at this point. "Maybe a little nervous or in a hurry like Mr. Hayes?"

Rudy folded his arms over his chest and rubbed his chin as he considered the question. "The usual Monday morning crowd came through. And they're all always in a hurry." He shook his head. "I'll never understand why working folks wait until Monday morning to fill up their gas tanks and then they complain because they're running late."

"Did anyone stop in that you didn't recognize?" Patrick asked. "Maybe someone in more of a hurry than the rest?"

Rudy shrugged. "There's always a few

strangers passing through. Usually not that many early in the morning. No one at all that I noticed today. Just the regulars."

"If you could provide us with a list of the regulars who were in this morning that would be useful." Patrick slid the request into the conversation, the maneuver slick as glass.

Bree noted the mounting confusion on Rudy's face. "I know that's asking a lot, Mr. Johnson, but we…" she glanced at Patrick, he gave her no indication not to proceed "…discovered a body in the park this morning. We have reason to believe some aspect of the crime was carried out between seven and eight this morning. So anyone you or your regulars might have seen in the area could be a person of interest in the case."

Rudy squared his shoulders and lifted his chin as if ready to do battle. "The regulars who come through my store are good people. Not criminals." The firm set of his jaw warned more so than his words that his hackles were up. "If any one of them had seen or heard anything I would know it."

"That may be," Patrick cut in, his tone firmer this time, "but we'll need that list all the same. Choosing not to provide the names constitutes obstruction of justice."

So much for congeniality. "Anything anyone may have seen could prove immensely helpful to our investigation," Bree explained, hoping to head off a complete lockdown. The Ute people were a proud, stubborn lot.

Despite having been raised here, Patrick apparently didn't understand that as a white man his imposing tone and words could come across the wrong way when dealing with a Ute man.

Rudy glared at Patrick a moment before turning his attention to Bree. "I'll give you the list if it's that important."

Patrick's own hackles visibly reared. His jaw tightened and the rigid set of his shoulders announced this loudly.

"Sheriff Martinez and I are working together," Bree clarified. "Your cooperation with the both of us will make our job a lot easier."

Rudy gave a single curt nod.

Bree pushed a smile into place, relieved. "Great. I'll pick up the list later today, if that's all right. I know you're busy."

Another tight nod.

"Thank you, Mr. Johnson," Bree offered, understanding that the man's continued cooperation depended a great deal on her keeping the lines of communication on a level that fostered mutual respect. As much as she hated to admit it, that was the very reason she would have no choice but to work directly with Patrick to some degree as long as they were a part of this investigation.

These people knew and trusted her. She was one of them. Patrick represented those who looked down at the Ute people. Unfairly lumped them all in the same category. There was good and bad in all people. No one liked to be judged wrongly because of the actions of others.

Patrick and Rudy exchanged one of those male half-nods that was barely civil.

At the front of the store Lizzy O'Dell was braced against the counter, busily filing her nails. Bree asked her the same questions they'd asked Rudy. Lizzy had been too busy at the register, she claimed, to notice anything out of the ordinary. Bree thanked her as well and made a path toward the door.

If she could get out of here without—

"Say hello to Peter for me," Rudy called after her.

Bree managed a decent stab at a smile and assured the man she would. She was out the door and climbing into her vehicle two steps ahead of Patrick in hopes of moving on before any related questions could be posed.

"Who's Peter?"

If she hadn't known that it was physically impossible for her heart to completely stop beating while she continued to breathe, Bree would have sworn that it had done just that.

As if luck had opted to show mercy, her cell phone vibrated. Saved by her cell twice in one morning.

"Excuse me." She pulled the phone from her belt and checked the screen.

Her sister. Tabitha.

The heart she'd been certain had stalled rammed into her sternum.

Bree didn't give any excuses to her passenger. She shoved the door open and stepped away from the vehicle for privacy.

"Hunter." Old habits were hard to change. Though she'd known it was her sister calling she answered in cop mode.

"Sis, I have to run some errands today. Do you need me to pick up Peter after school?"

Bree glanced back at her vehicle. Patrick remained in the passenger seat. Though he stared straight ahead she knew better than to believe he wasn't keeping tabs on her movements.

"That would be great. Today's going to be a long one." Bree took a few more steps away from the vehicle. "I don't have much time but we need to talk."

"Uh-oh. What's wrong?"

Her sister knew her well. Another covert glance at her SUV to ensure Patrick was still seated inside with the windows up. Bree lowered her voice to scarcely more than a whisper. "Peter asked me about his father this morning. He wouldn't let it go."

"I've been telling you for years that this conversation—"

"Yeah, yeah, I know," Bree interrupted. She didn't need to hear this right now. Irritation gnawed at her. "I just don't need any help from you and Layla making that happen sooner rather than later. He overheard something Layla said about his father being as bad as Jack."

The silence on the other end of the line told Bree that her sister realized the mistake.

"Oh, Bree, I'm sorry. Layla was complaining about Patrick's deputies singling out teenage drivers. She was off on a *profiling* tangent. She made that remark out of frustration. She didn't mean it and certainly neither of us intended for Peter to overhear."

Bree closed her eyes and let out a weary breath. "It's okay. Just tell Layla to be more careful. I can't deal with that issue—" she snuck another look at the man in question "—not right now."

"Is something going on?"

"We'll talk about it later," Bree promised. Patrick would be growing impatient. "I have to get back to work. Take care of my boy for me, okay?"

"You know I will. And Bree…"

"Yeah."

"Be careful out there. Peter needs you. We all need you."

Bree promised Tabitha she would use caution and ended the call. Her family had worried about her since she'd decided to go into law enforcement, but lately Tabitha had worried a little extra. And it was Bree's fault. She should never have told her sister about the other night. But she'd needed to tell someone.

Bree had been getting those weird feelings…the ones that warned someone was watching her or following her. She would be certain she'd glimpsed someone in her peripheral vision, but she hadn't actually caught anyone yet. It always turned out to be nothing. Then, night before last, she'd been certain someone followed her home. Maybe it was nothing. Coincidence, paranoia, whatever. Yet as a trained cop she knew better than to assume her instincts were completely off the mark.

Ignoring danger, real or imagined, could cost a lot more than she wanted to pay.

Like she'd told Tabitha, Bree didn't have time to deal with that right now, either. She strode back to the SUV and climbed behind the wheel.

"Sorry 'bout that," she said to Patrick. She almost…*almost* stated out loud that she'd needed to make arrangements for her son. Damn. He was so much a part of her life talking about him was like breathing.

"No problem."

She'd just started the vehicle and shifted into Reverse when he said, "So, who's Peter?"

THE KENNER COUNTY Crime Unit was housed on the top floor of the old city annex building on the outskirts of Kenner City. The building had been used as storage for retired files as long as Bree could remember. When the Bureau finally authorized a crime lab for the Four Corners area the third floor was the only space the city would forfeit. But that didn't stop Callie MacBride and her team from carving out a pretty impressive reputation. Like the little engine that could.

Bree was relieved to be joining the others for the briefing. The better part of six hours spent with Patrick Martinez had her emotions raw. They'd been to her office and to his. They'd stopped at every business within a ten-mile radius of the park entrance. And they'd picked up the list from Rudy Johnson. Bree recognized the majority of the names on the list. Chances were it would be a dead end.

Busywork—that's what they had been doing all day. With next to nothing to go on they'd started with the most elementary procedure: question anyone and everyone in the vicinity of the crime.

Bree was certain that Patrick, as sheriff of Kenner County, had numerous other duties he could have been attending to. Any one of his deputies could have worked with her. But no, he'd stuck close to her all day.

To ferret out information. She was certain. Why did he care what she'd been up to for the past eight years? Her life was none of his business. She'd told him so when he'd pressed the issue of "who's Peter?" and "is that your husband?"

Her nerves were shot.

The entire time her sister's voice had kept echoing in the back of her mind… *You should come clean with both Peter and Patrick. This decision will come back to haunt you.* Although Bree's father had insisted it was her decision, her older sister had staunchly disagreed from the beginning.

Bottom line, Bree couldn't undo the past. She'd made her decision. There was no changing it now. Frustration expanded inside her. So far she'd seen no real reason to regret the decisions she'd made.

Patrick Martinez's nosiness definitely wasn't a good reason.

Inside the annex, Bree and Patrick took the stairs to the third floor. She could feel his gaze on her with every step she took. Or maybe it was her imagination. He'd been dissecting everything she'd done all day. Every word. Every move.

Thank God this day was almost over.

On the third floor, Bree stopped at the receptionist's desk. She dredged up a smile. "We're here for the briefing on the Grainger investigation."

"Detective Hunter?" The receptionist, Elizabeth Reddawn according to the name-plate on her desk, returned Bree's smile.

"That's right." Bree gestured to Patrick. "And Sheriff Martinez."

"Good afternoon, Sheriff." Elizabeth's smile widened. "We've set up a command center in the conference room down the hall," she told Patrick. "You know, the one that used to be a storage room?"

"I know the way," Patrick confirmed. "Thanks, Elizabeth."

Bree should have realized that Patrick worked directly with the lab on a regular basis. He would know the personnel and his way around. Bree, on the other hand, usually got her feedback from the lab through the chain-of-command channels at TPD. She rarely had the opportunity to work directly with anyone at the lab, except, on the rare occasion, Callie MacBride.

Though ten minutes early for the meeting, the conference-room-turned-command-center was crowded with what Bree suspected were FBI agents. She didn't recognize any other local law enforcement personnel.

Special Agent in Charge Jerry Ortiz turned to greet Patrick and Bree as they entered the room.

"Patrick." Ortiz shook his hand. "Detective Hunter, I presume." He reached for Bree's next.

"Ortiz, this is Detective Sabrina Hunter," Patrick said, making the formal introduction, "from Towaoc PD."

"I'm pleased to have you on our team,

Detective Hunter," Ortiz said with all the panache of a politician. To Patrick he said, "I decided to come in personally to handle…this." He exhaled a heavy breath. "That's the least I can do."

"Completely understandable," Patrick confirmed.

Bree had heard Ortiz's name on a number of occasions, not to mention she'd seen him in the news on a regular basis. He was assigned to the Bureau field office in Durango.

"Let's take our seats," Ortiz announced to the room at large. He stood behind the chair at the head of the conference table.

Bree put some distance between Patrick and herself. She needed a breather. She settled into a chair next to Callie.

When the room had settled, Ortiz made the necessary introductions. Some of those present Bree recognized from various homicide cases she'd worked. She'd rarely interacted with them, but she was familiar with the faces. Some had been at the crime scene that morning, like O'Shea, Fleming and Miguel Acevedo. Steven Griswold, an older gentleman who was the lab's firearms expert, she hadn't seen before. Olivia Perez and Jacob Webster. Bree had seen those two around town at lunch together more than once, but she'd never run into either one in the field. She wondered if they were a couple. No wedding rings that she could see, but a definite connection. Every shared glance screamed of that connection.

Three of the field agents present Bree couldn't recall having run into before. FBI agents Tom Ryan, Ben Parrish and Dylan Acevedo. According to Ortiz, Tom Ryan and Dylan Acevedo had flown straight here from their home offices upon hearing the news. That would explain why she didn't recognize any of the three.

Whoa! Dylan Acevedo looked so much like Miguel. Considering they shared the same last name, they had to be brothers.

As if Agent Ortiz had read her mind, he said, "For those of you who don't know, the Acevedo brothers are twins." Ortiz gestured vaguely. "I noted the confusion on some faces so I thought I'd better clear that up before we get started."

Bree hoped she wasn't the only one who'd been confused. Across the table Patrick glanced at her. Oh yeah, she was the only one. Great.

"We all know why we're here," Ortiz said somberly. "Special Agent Julie Grainger will be sorely missed. There are no adequate words to articulate how we all feel about this loss. But anger and regret won't help Agent Grainger and it won't assist us in what we have to do. There is one final thing we can do to support our fallen colleague and that is to ensure her murderer is brought to justice in the speediest possible manner. With that in mind, I'd like to share what I can with all those present regarding her latest case.

"Considering the nature of the investigation in which she was involved, we have good reason to believe that case may be the motive behind her murder."

Tension rifled through Bree. The Bureau

wasn't always so forthcoming with local law enforcement, at least not at this level. But everyone present wanted this crime solved—fast.

"This briefing," Ortiz went on, "is need-to-know only. Any leaks could jeopardize the homicide investigation. I don't have to spell it out. Though the Bureau will be handling the main thrust of the investigation, support from the sheriff's department as well as other local police departments will greatly enhance our ability to get the job done under the circumstances."

Around the long conference table the faces remained grim but the determination to do just as Ortiz suggested was thick in the air.

"For several months," Ortiz went on, "Agent Grainger has been investigating the disappearance and whereabouts of Vincent Del Gardo."

Next to Bree, Callie MacBride caught her breath. The sound was so soft Bree was reasonably sure she was the only one to hear it. From the corner of her eye Bree studied Callie. Her face had gone deathly pale, her features even tighter with tension.

Before Bree could analyze the reaction, Ortiz drew her attention once more.

"...based in Las Vegas, Vincent is the head of the Del Gardo crime family. Nearly three years ago he escaped custody and we've been trying to find him ever since. Agent Grainger, after months of intensive work, had tracked him to the Four Corners area."

Bree tried not to let her attention drift back to the woman beside her, but it was hard not to. As Callie reached up to tuck her hair behind her ear, her hand shook. Bree reminded herself that Callie and Grainger may have been very close friends as well as colleagues. Her reaction might simply be stronger than most due to the personal connection.

"Agent Grainger's investigation had revealed that Del Gardo had purchased a large estate in the area. Unfortunately, before we could close in on him, the estate was sold to a civilian, Griffin Vaughn, who has no ties to Del Gardo. We can only assume, of course, at this point that Agent Grainger's death is somehow related to her investigation. But Del Gardo has a reputation for erasing any presumed nuisance in just this manner."

Ortiz leaned forward, braced his hands on the back of his chair. "We will get this bastard and whoever he hired to take down our agent and friend—one way or another. As badly as we want Del Gardo for many other reasons, right now our primary goal is to determine who murdered Agent Grainger."

The escalating tension seemed to press all the air out of the room. All present wanted to do exactly as Ortiz suggested. To find this killer. Now.

Ortiz briefly reviewed the few details they had on the Grainger investigation already. No real evidence had been discovered at the scene. The hope was that Grainger's body would reveal crucial evidence and lead them to her killer. At last Ortiz got to the 9-1-1 call.

"Are we ready to listen to the call?" he asked Callie.

She stiffened as if she'd been tugged from deep thought, then cleared her throat. "Yes." She gestured to Olivia. "As you may have already heard," the lab's head forensic scientist began as she stood and cleared her throat again, "Burt Hayes, a Ute guide at the Tribal Park, found…the body and made a call to the Towaoc Police Department. During that same time the county's 9-1-1 system received a call as well. This one from a male caller who did not identify himself."

A flurry of movement and muttered words at the other end of the long table drew the room's collective attention there.

Agent Parrish shot to his feet, as did Agent Tom Ryan.

"Sorry. I… I'm all thumbs today," Parrish stammered. He grabbed his overturned coffee cup. Mopped at the spill with a lone napkin.

"It's all right." Ryan waved his hands as if erasing the incident. "We're all out of

sorts today. Anyway, you're the one who caught the spill."

Coffee had dripped onto Parrish's khaki slacks.

"Excuse me." He shook his head in disgust. "I'll… I'll be right back. Tom can bring me…up to speed," he said to Ortiz and the room at large as he hurried toward the door.

Ortiz didn't look pleased but carried on. "Let's hear that recording."

Callie nodded to Olivia, who pressed the necessary buttons to play the recorded call.

The 9-1-1 operator's practiced greeting resonated first. A moment of silence. Then, "I need to report a…murder." The voice sounded distant, as if the mouthpiece of the phone was too far away or partially covered. Some muffled sounds and something like, "Oh, God." The male voice continued, "At the Ute Reservation Tribal Park…the body's…oh, God." During the silence that followed, the operator asked the caller to identify himself and that he provide additional details. The caller severed the connection.

As the recording ended the room remained dead silent.

Agent Tom Ryan abruptly pushed out of his chair. "Play that again."

Callie stiffened.

Bree studied first the woman beside her, who seemed suddenly even more flustered, then the man. The cold fury on his face was different than before…had moved to a new level.

Olivia obliged and replayed the recording. Not a single word was uttered by anyone present as the clearly emotional caller's voice filled the air. There was something familiar about his voice, Bree realized this time. The first time she'd been focused on the information relayed. This time she analyzed the voice. Bree knew that voice. Had heard it before.

As the recording ended Agent Parrish reentered the room. That was when Bree recalled where and when she'd heard that voice.

"It was you."

Bree's gaze snapped to the woman next to her.

"You made the call," Callie said, the accusation directed at Agent Ben Parrish.

Agent Ryan stared at the man who'd stalled halfway back to his chair. "What's going on here, Ben?"

All hell broke loose then.

Dylan Acevedo and Parrish almost came to blows. Patrick and Jacob pulled the men apart with Ortiz's assistance.

The already suffocating tension in the room rocketed to a whole other stratosphere even as Ortiz demanded order. The silence that instantly replaced the chaos was even more unnerving.

What was going on here? Bree couldn't believe what she was hearing and seeing. Agent Parrish had discovered the body? Why would he conceal that fact? Why had he left the scene?

"You want to explain this?" Ortiz suggested, his voice hoarse from shouting.

Whatever was going on with the three

agents at the other end of the table wasn't good. Bree's first thought was that if Parrish was guilty of something he could have made a run for it as soon as he realized the 9-1-1 recording would be played. But he hadn't. He'd come back into the room knowing what he would face.

"I received a text message," Parrish explained, his tone emotionless, exhausted, "that I should meet Julie this morning." He shrugged, his shoulders rounded with the weight of his confession. "The number the text came from raised my suspicions immediately since it showed up as unknown. Julie's number is on my contact list. And when I sent a text asking her to call me it was ignored." He grabbed the edge of the table to steady himself.

"I hadn't heard from her in weeks and I wasn't about to risk ignoring the request. I was aware that she was deep into her investigation." He heaved a heavy breath. "I figured she needed me and had used whatever means available to contact me.

So I went. And…" He dragged a ragged breath into his lungs. "She was dead. Had been for a couple of days."

"And you didn't call it in and stay with her?" Ryan demanded. "What the hell were you thinking? How could you leave her like that?"

"What's the motive?" Dylan demanded. "Why would anyone send you a text to meet her? That doesn't make sense. Why you? You're not involved in the Del Gardo investigation."

More of that consuming silence pressed in on Bree's chest as everyone in the room waited for Parrish to give a reasonable explanation for his actions.

Parrish shook his head. "I don't know. I can only assume it was a setup." He looked around the room. "One that appears to have worked."

The tension between the three agents erupted into another heated exchange, only this time without the physical tactics.

"Enough!" Ortiz commanded. He held up his hands and waited for silence.

The glare-off between Ryan, Parrish and the visiting Acevedo brother would have cut through steel.

"We will get to the bottom of this," Ortiz promised. His openly suspicious gaze nailed Parrish. "We'll start by having you turn over your cell phone, Agent. If there's any chance we can trace the number where that text came from, we might have a starting place."

Parrish tossed his cell onto the table. "Be my guest. I have nothing to hide." He said the last sentence with considerably less conviction than the first.

"Yeah, right," Dylan muttered.

Ortiz let his glare speak for itself. When the moment had passed, he doled out assignments. "Detective Hunter," he said as his attention rested on Bree, "talk to your contacts among the Ute reservation residents. See if anyone has heard any rumblings regarding the murder of a federal agent. Someone, somewhere will have heard something."

"Yes, sir." Bree could definitely do that.

The murder of a federal agent was a major deal, even in Colorado's so-called murder capital. There would be gossip.

Ortiz gave Patrick the same basic order. The agents in the room would attempt to reconstruct Grainger's activities to date. Another briefing would be scheduled in forty-eight hours or sooner if necessary.

As the meeting was dismissed, Bree watched the agents fall into their respective groups. Callie and her lab team huddled to discuss strategy. Agents Tom Ryan and Dylan Acevedo spoke quietly but tensely with Ortiz.

Ben Parrish stood alone, accused and outside the circle of his peers. Bree didn't know the guy, but she couldn't help feeling a little sorry for him. Surely if he was guilty of wrongdoing he'd have made a run for it. To stand here and face all this…it was hard.

But then, she didn't know him. The one thing she did know was that time would tell. If Parrish was involved with Grainger's murder, given time, the investigation would nail him.

The lab folks began to filter from the room. When Callie would have followed her team Tom Ryan stopped her at the door. Callie had been visibly stressed to the max all through the briefing, but her reaction to Ryan was different. The same fierce tension but with another layer. Bree couldn't quite pinpoint it, but there was definite tension between the two that transcended the case.

"I guess you'll have to give me a ride back to my vehicle."

Patrick's voice tugged Bree from her disturbing musings. "Sure." The sooner she was free of his constant analysis the better.

She made her way out of the building and to her SUV. Stopping by the office before going home was essential. She would have messages and she needed to put some of her conclusions into notes. And she wanted to see what she could find on Parrish, if anything.

"I was thinking," Patrick said as they loaded into her SUV.

She could pretend not to hear him but he'd only repeat himself. "Thinking what?" That he couldn't wait to be rid of her? If so, they were on the same page.

"We should coordinate our efforts. There's a lot about this investigation that will fall under Bureau domain and we won't be privy to. But what we can do is put out feelers, follow up on any leads and rattle cages. That effort would be far better served if we work at it jointly."

So much for going her own way.

She'd spent the last eight years attempting to put the past behind her. Now the primary part she'd tried to avoid was smack dab in the middle of her present.

And there wasn't any way to avoid the momentum-gaining collision she felt with every fiber of her being was barreling her way.

Chapter Four

Bree parked in front of her sister's home and shut off the engine. She was exhausted. Mentally more so than physically. She leaned against the headrest and closed her eyes.

How was she going to get through this?

It was bad enough a member of law enforcement was dead, but being joined at the hip with Patrick for the duration of the investigation was nearly more than she could bear.

After eight years she'd hoped the past wasn't going to catch up to her.

Boy, had she been wrong.

She opened her eyes and peered at her sister's home. Her son was waiting for her.

She couldn't keep sitting out here trying to pull herself together. She had to go inside and pretend that she hadn't spent the day with the father he didn't know.

That she wasn't lying to him for her own selfish reasons.

And she wasn't…was she?

"No more stalling."

She climbed out of her SUV and trudged up the front walk, then the steps. It was dark and she was so tired. Maybe a long, hot bath and some quality time with her son would rejuvenate her.

Tabitha met her at the door, her face clouded with worry as always. "Are you okay? That federal agent's murder has been all over the news this evening. Is that the case you're working on?"

Bree nodded, hoped her sister didn't ask any more than that. She couldn't talk about the investigation and she didn't want to talk about having to spend time with Patrick.

"I'll bet you haven't eaten all day." Tabitha took hold of Bree's arm and tugged her inside. "I'll warm you up some soup. Peter's already eaten and done his homework. He's watching TV with Layla."

Before Bree could ask, Tabitha tacked on, "And don't worry. Layla and I talked. There won't be any more discussions about you know who."

Bree appreciated that. "Thanks, sis."

The door had scarcely closed behind her when Peter rushed to give his mom a hug. Bree missed her son so when a day dragged on and on like this one. She mussed his dark hair and kissed the top of his head. "I hope you've been good for your aunt Tabitha."

Peter dragged his mom to the kitchen table and reviewed his day's work with her while Tabitha warmed up the soup. Peter was not only a talented little artist he was a bright pupil. His work ethic and grades continued to make her proud. He was such a good boy.

But he was growing up. Before long he wouldn't want to share his schoolwork with her, much less talk about his day.

Maybe she had made a mistake. He yearned so for a man in his life. His uncle Roy tried to be there for him but Tabitha's husband worked for an oil company and spent more time away from home than not.

When Peter had been a baby and then a toddler, Bree had been totally convinced that her decision was the right one. But after what she'd gone through with Jack and now as she watched her son grow into a young man, she questioned every decision she had made.

By the time Peter had been drawn back to the television by his favorite show, Tabitha had placed a bowl of steaming potato soup along with a glass of chocolate milk in front of Bree.

"Eat," her sister ordered. "And tell me what I can do to clear those worry lines from your face. You make me worry." She scrubbed at her brow. "And God knows I don't need any more lines."

Bree had to smile, even if only a little. Her sister had taken over the role of mother after their mom had died. Bree had been only fourteen. Four years older, Tabitha had put off going to college to stay home and help their father raise Bree. College had gone by the wayside permanently when Tabitha met Roy. Love at first sight. But Tabitha's had been a good choice. She had a wonderful husband who treated her with respect.

Bree picked up her spoon and stirred her soup. She really had no appetite. Who could eat when she kept thinking about Julie Grainger lying alone in that desolate place for two days before she was found.

"What worry?" Bree countered her sister's suggestion. "I have no worries."

Tabitha rolled her eyes. "Uh-huh, that's right. Denial. They have therapy and drugs for that disorder, little sister."

Bree might as well come clean. Tabitha had ways of prying until she dug up the truth. She was relentless when she picked up the scent of something. Why waste the energy trying to outmaneuver her?

After a quick check to see that Peter was

fully occupied with the TV, Bree spilled her guts. She carefully worded each revealing statement so that even if her son did overhear something he'd have no idea who she was talking about.

"You were with him the entire day?"

Bree nodded and forced a spoonful of her favorite soup past her lips. She didn't feel hungry but she recognized the need to refuel her body. The next few days and weeks would require all the strength she could muster.

Tabitha chewed her lip thoughtfully. "You know what this means, don't you?"

Bree wasn't sure she wanted to hear her sister's assessment. "A pain in the butt, that's what I know it means."

Tabitha dismissed that explanation with a wave of her hands. "It means he still has feelings for you." Before Bree could protest that statement, Tabitha went on, "He's using this case as an excuse to get close to you again. To find out what you've been up to all these years. Like you said, he could assign one of his deputies to work with you."

All these years. Bree was sick to death of thinking about all these years. "This isn't an episode of your favorite soap. This is real life and the case is why we're stuck together. My guess is that if he's really as curious as he seems it's only because he wants to hear how miserable my life has been. Men are like that." She licked her spoon and pointed it at her sister. "They want to believe your life is crap without them even if they don't want to be in your life. It's some sort of genetic obsession."

Tabitha arched an eyebrow in objection.

"Okay," Bree allowed, "so Roy is different. He's perfect. But most men are exactly that way. Take Jack—" Bree craned her neck to get a look into the living room "—his goal in life was to make me miserable. Then when I'd had enough he wanted me to be even more miserable without him. He's even had the nerve to try and get me back."

Jack had been her second big mistake. Her father had been certain Bree would be happier with a Ute man as a husband and to raise her young son. Too bad she'd picked one of the bad guys. Giving herself credit, even her family had been fooled at first.

Jackson Raintree had earned his nickname, Big Jack the Bully, many times over. He was an abusive, alcoholic jerk who had no respect for women or people in general. He was nothing but a user. Why, oh, why hadn't she seen that before it was too late? Maybe because she had a young son who needed a father figure? Jack pretended to respect her work…made her think he believed she could do anything. But he'd lied. And she'd fallen for it.

In truth maybe she'd just needed to forget the past. She'd hoped that learning to care about someone else would help erase Patrick Martinez from her heart once and for all.

She'd gotten neither.

"I think you're wrong," Tabitha argued. She checked her fingernails as if assessing whether or not she needed a manicure. "I've sort of kept up with Patrick over the years."

Bree's head snapped up. "What?" This was the first she'd heard of that. "Why would you do that?"

No longer able to avoid eye contact using her cuticles as an excuse, Tabitha's gaze settled on Bree's. "I didn't want Peter to lose all that time."

"What does that mean?" Bree didn't know whether to be angry or worried.

"Bring your soup," Tabitha order, "and come with me."

Curious or maybe scared of what her sister may have been doing *all these years,* Bree did as she was told. Soup bowl in hand, she followed Tabitha up the stairs and to her bedroom.

"Sit." Tabitha gestured to the bed.

Bree sat and, having forgotten her spoon, sipped her soup straight from the bowl. She had a feeling she was going to need refueling more than she'd thought.

Tabitha dug around on the top shelf of her closet and pulled out a box. She sat on the bed next to Bree and opened it. Inside was a thick, leather-bound album or scrapbook. Bree's heart rate accelerated. This was…unbelievable.

"I started it when Peter was about one."

As Tabitha flipped through the pages each breath grew more difficult for Bree to draw in. Newspaper clippings from what appeared to be every single time the sheriff had been spotlighted. The dates went all the way back to when he'd first taken the remainder of the former sheriff's term. Patrick had been brought in to clean up the department. He'd gotten the job done and more. The citizens of Kenner County loved him.

Old snapshots of Bree and Patrick together were tucked into pages that included handwritten captions. Emotions Bree couldn't begin to label churned inside her.

"I threw those photos out." Bree's words were scarcely a whisper. "Years ago."

"I—" Tabitha wet her lips "—dug them out of your trash can and kept them."

"My God." Bree shook her head as she moved through more of the pages.

"He never married, Bree. He works all the time. That has to mean something."

Bree met her sister's hopeful gaze. She didn't know how to respond to that.

"Please don't be mad at me. I was so afraid you would regret erasing your past that way. Someday you'll need these mementos. Peter will need them."

Too overwhelmed to speak, Bree didn't know whether to hug her sister or to slug her. She dragged her attention from the old memories. "I honestly don't know how I feel about this, but I understand why you did it."

"I guess that's enough for now," Tabitha offered, tears shining in her eyes. "Remember, no matter how you feel about him, he's still the father of your son and you love your son. The time will come when you can't pretend anymore that Peter's father doesn't exist."

Bree was terrified that that time had come already.

After getting her emotions in check, Bree rounded up her son and his things and headed for her vehicle. Tabitha followed her onto the porch.

"I'll just plan to pick Peter up after school until you tell me different," Tabitha offered.

What would Bree do without her? "Thanks." She hugged her sister, couldn't bring herself to let go for a bit.

"Oh, my God." Tabitha drew back abruptly, her eyes wide with horror.

"What's wrong?" Her sister's gaze was fixed on something behind Bree…something in the street.

"Mommy, what happened to your car?"

Bree jerked around. Several moments were required for her brain to adequately assess what her eyes saw.

The words painted in ugly black across the silver of her SUV shook her, made her knees weak.

I'm watching you.

PATRICK SCRUBBED the towel over his head to dry his hair. He felt a hundred percent better after his shower. The day had been too grating on his senses. Had left them raw and stinging.

Julie Grainger's murder had set the tone, tearing at his soul. But running headlong into Bree on the case had kept his emotions in turmoil all damned day.

He'd told himself a thousand times over that he no longer cared and then he got a glimpse of her in town or on one of those rare, self-defeating occasions when he drove by her house late at night and the lie was revealed.

He'd never gotten over her. Maybe if he'd tried harder…had given any other woman a chance…

When he'd heard Bree had gotten married, he'd thought that was it. He could move on and put that part of his life behind him. Even then he'd still longed for her. Today, watching her, smelling that unique scent of hers and hearing her voice…he'd known for certain he would never stop loving her.

He was a fool. She was married. She belonged to another man. He had no right feeling those emotions. He damned sure had no right allowing her to recognize his feelings. He had a bad feeling he'd let her catch him watching her one time too many.

One way or another he had to keep reminding himself that she belonged to someone else.

But she hadn't been wearing a wedding ring. And she still used her maiden name. Did that mean she was no longer with the other man?

Damn him for wondering.

Patrick tossed the towel aside and tugged on a T-shirt. He needed to eat and get some sleep. He had work to do at the office first thing in the morning before meeting Bree for lunch to go over any leads either of them had discovered.

He'd picked the Morning Ray Café, his mom's diner, for their meeting. Seemed a safe enough spot to spend time with Bree in neutral territory. He would have the home field advantage and his mom would hover close, ensuring Patrick stayed on his toes.

His cell rattled against the counter and

Patrick snatched it up. Getting a call at this time of night was never a good thing.

"Martinez."

"Sheriff, I hope I'm not calling you too late."

Clayton Mitchell, his personal assistant. Clayton preferred to be called a personal assistant rather than a secretary. Patrick couldn't care less what he wanted to be called. Clayton was a man but he was the best damned secretary Patrick had ever had.

"It's never too late to call if you feel the need," Patrick reminded him. "What's up?"

As he waited for his assistant to get to the point of his call, Patrick padded barefoot into the kitchen to browse the offerings in the fridge.

"When I came to work for you…" Clayton began.

Oh, hell. Patrick sure hoped he wasn't about to lose his assistant. He was pretty sure he couldn't stay on top of things without him. In the five years since Clayton had come on board Patrick's professional life had gone from stressful to organized and reasonably relaxed—for a lawman.

"Clayton, if you're bucking for a raise, you know I'll have to run it by the—"

"Sheriff," Clayton cut him off, his tone testy, "this isn't about a raise."

"Oh." Patrick frowned. "Well, then, go ahead with whatever you were going to say."

He snagged a beer from the fridge and some leftover lasagna his mother had sent home with him.

"Now that you mention it, though," Clayton countered, "I could use a raise."

Patrick shook his head. "Get to the point. Now that you've mentioned it, it is getting late."

The sigh that hissed across the line was completely exaggerated. "Anyway, when you hired me you said there were two things I was never to bring up. Your lack of a social life and Sabrina Hunter."

Damn. Had word that he was working

with Bree gotten out around the department already?

"That's right," Patrick confirmed. "I hope you're not about to fall down on your word after all this time. You do have a job performance evaluation coming up."

Another of those dramatic sighs. "Normally I wouldn't dream of going against your wishes, but I just heard something from a friend that I thought you might need to know since you're working with Detective Hunter on the Grainger homicide."

Friend? Patrick's frown deepened to a scowl, the furrows of frustration dragged at his brow. "What on God's green earth are you talking about?"

"Jesse Phillips, who works dispatch over at Towaoc Police Department, just called and told me a call came in requesting assistance. The call was from Detective Sabrina Hunter."

Adrenaline charged through Patrick's veins. "What address?"

Clayton spouted off the address. Patrick

had to think a moment. Tabitha's house. Bree's sister. "What kind of assistance?" Patrick demanded.

"That," Clayton said, "I don't know. But I thought you needed to be aware there might be a problem. Detective Hunter specifically asked that the call not go out over dispatch lines."

Which was code for Bree didn't want anyone to know whatever the hell was going on at her sister's residence. Damn.

"Thanks, Clayton. I'll check it out."

Patrick ended the call and pulled on his shoes. He grabbed his jacket and keys and headed for the door.

His pulse wouldn't slow even as he ordered himself to take deep, controlled breaths. Bree knew how to take care of herself. But her sister could be hurt. There may have been trouble at her house.

Whatever the hell it was, he intended to find out for certain that everyone was all right.

Half an hour later Patrick took the final turn onto the street where Tabitha lived. A small neighborhood in the Towaoc area with neat rows of housing that rose a cut above the norm. She and her husband, Roy, had done well for themselves.

Bree's SUV was parked in front along with two other vehicles. Patrick caught a glimpse of her talking to two men, one wearing a TPD uniform. When Patrick parked next to the curb he could see that the guy wearing civilian clothes was Steve Cyrus from the homicide scene that morning. Patrick didn't recognize the uniformed officer.

That Bree appeared to be all right sent relief gushing through him. Patrick emerged from his SUV and headed across the quiet street.

Bree's gaze collided with his and she looked away. She tucked her cell phone against her ear so he assumed she'd gotten a call.

"Cyrus," Patrick said as he approached the two men, "what's going on?"

Cyrus glanced at Bree before responding. Since she was busy with her call, he gestured to her vehicle. "Someone vandalized Detective Hunter's SUV. We've checked for prints already, but you know how these things go. There are literally dozens. And the chances of catching the perpetrator is not very likely."

Patrick walked to the side of the SUV closest to the house. The oxygen stalled in his chest when he read the words painted there.

I'm watching you.

"Is this the first incident of this nature Detective Hunter has experienced?"

"Yes, sir." Cyrus glanced at Bree once more. She'd put away her cell phone. "To the best of my knowledge it is."

When Bree joined the huddle, Cyrus said, "We've done all we can, Detective Hunter. We'll run this to the lab first thing in the morning and ask them to put a rush on the database comparison."

"Thanks, Cyrus." Bree looked from Cyrus to Patrick. "What're you doing here, Patrick?"

Cyrus hitched a thumb toward what

was obviously his vehicle. "I'll talk to you tomorrow."

Bree watched Cyrus and Officer Day leave. Patrick waited until he had her full attention. "What's going on with this?" He indicated her SUV.

Bree looked anywhere but at him. "It's probably kids. You know how it is around here. Not enough of the right kind of activities to keep them occupied. Mom and Dad both work too many hours and—"

"That's crap," Patrick rebutted. "You won't look me in the eye and we both know that warnings like that don't generally come from restless teenagers. This is personal, Bree. What the hell is going on?"

With obvious reluctance, she met his gaze. "I'm a cop, Patrick. You know how this works. I make enemies every other day. Sometimes they like getting even." She gestured to her SUV. "This is getting even."

"Has anything else like this happened lately?"

More of that hesitation. "Look, this is

none of your business, Patrick. I don't know how you found out about this, but you can go home now. We've got the situation under control."

She had a point there. He couldn't deny it. This was none of his business. But that didn't prevent him from getting mad as hell. If something was going on, he wanted to know what was being done about it besides lifting a few latent prints.

"We're working together on a high priority homicide case," he reminded her. "If something's going on in your personal life that might affect your job performance or my safety when in your presence, I have a right to know." He was reaching but right now he didn't care as long as he got the truth out of her.

"I can't believe this." Bree planted her hands on her hips, her mouth agape with disbelief or something like it. "Are you seriously trying to strong-arm me into telling you my personal business? You should watch your step, Patrick. There are rules against this sort of thing."

He didn't have to think about it. "That's exactly what I'm doing." He matched her stance, hands fixed at his waist. "No more games, Bree. Tell me what's really going on here."

She had the darkest eyes. Standing here beneath the streetlight he couldn't help but notice. He'd noticed way too much today already. But, evidently, in her presence he was helpless not to inventory the details he'd missed so damned much for so damned long.

She peered up at him. He watched the struggle in those dark eyes. She didn't want to tell him. Whatever it was, she didn't want him to know.

Whatever crazy brain cell misfired at that moment he couldn't say but the next thing he knew he'd grabbed her by the shoulders and given her a little shake. "The truth. I want the truth."

That was the moment when he knew that the answers he wanted had nothing to do with her vandalized vehicle and every-thing to do with their past. Why had she walked away without giving him another chance? Better yet, why had he let her?

"I've gotten a few strange calls," she relented. "Always from phones in public places." She moistened her lips and his throat ached. "Lately I've felt like someone has been following me, but then there wouldn't be anyone there." She pulled free of his grasp. "It's probably nothing." The vulnerability in her eyes vanished. "Besides, I'm a big girl, Sheriff. I don't need you taking care of me."

And therein lay the rub. Their relationship had ended because he was too protective. Too controlling of her career decisions.

This was different.

He didn't care what she said. He knew the signs. Chances were she had a stalker. Either an admirer or, as she'd said before, an enemy. Neither one was a good thing.

"You have two choices here, Bree." The fury kindled once more. "You can work with me on this or I'll speak to your chief about it. Take your pick."

That was playing dirty. He understood that, but he wasn't about to let her ignore the warning signs. Stalkers, whether admirers or enemies, injured or killed the objects of the obsessions far too often to take the risk.

"Damn, Patrick!" She stopped a moment, visibly attempted to calm herself. Apparently it didn't work. "You haven't changed a bit." She poked him in the chest with her forefinger. "I don't need you taking care of me. Do you hear me? I can take care of myself. You are no longer a part of my life." She blinked, swallowed hard. "So back off!"

He should have listened to her. Should have been ticked off at her insinuation. But all he could do was stare into those deep, deep brown eyes and wonder how he'd ever let this much time pass without touching her…tasting her.

A little voice, growing weaker by the second, kept reminding him that the last he'd heard she was married. That didn't stop him from going temporarily stupid and fulfilling the fantasies that had tortured him every night for eight long years.

He took her face in his hands before she could fathom his intent and kissed her square on the lips.

Inside, he melted, but outside…he hardened like a rock. She tasted like sweet chocolate and hot, tempting woman. He wanted to pull her close and tuck her soft curves into his hard body.

She banged on his chest. Pulled away. "Don't you dare," she warned.

Patrick shuddered with the overdose of emotions. He blinked, once, twice. What the hell was he doing?

He dropped his hands. Took a step back. "I'm…" Damn, how did he excuse such behavior? "I'm sorry. I guess I got carried away and lost my head."

Damned straight he'd lost his head.

He'd gone way too far.

Bree trembled. He cursed himself.

"Just go, Patrick." She sucked in a ragged breath. She squared her shoulders in an attempt to compose herself. "I'll see you at

Nora's for lunch tomorrow. We'll…" She shrugged, still visibly struggling to maintain her bearing. He'd shaken her. "We'll review what we have on the case and…"

"Fine." If she let him off the hook this easily he was damned lucky.

He'd definitely crossed the line.

"Well." She backed up another step. "Good night then."

He turned around, read those words scrawled across her vehicle once more and changed his mind.

Patrick faced her once more, met her expectant gaze. "You won't mind if I follow you home? Just to be safe."

He'd kissed her. As crazy as it sounded, he'd put himself at risk for legal action. Had acted like an idiot, basically. Whether it was the kiss or his overbearing tactics, whatever the reason Bree just stood there staring at him.

"Look." He turned his palms up, tried his best to sound humble. "I shouldn't have kissed you, that was way out of line. It won't happen again. But you've got a serious situation here." He gestured to her vandalized vehicle. "It's not like I'm asking you to invite me into your home."

Still she said nothing, just stared at him.

Well, hell.

"I'll take that as a yes." He started toward his SUV but called over his shoulder. "I'll be standing by. Whenever you're ready to go, I'll be right behind you."

Chapter Five

Bree peered at her reflection in the mirror.

What was she doing?

She'd gotten up this morning, taken her son to school and come to work as if nothing had changed.

From eight-thirty until noon she had worked diligently. She'd touched base with half a dozen reliable informants, called every name on Rudy's list and come up empty-handed. If anyone knew anything, they were too afraid to talk.

Not unusual. Just frustrating.

Now, at half past twelve, she stood in the ladies' room contemplating how she looked.

"This is bad."

One day had changed everything. Put

her entire existence into a tailspin. Last night had been the no-turning-back point.

No matter how she lied to herself. No matter how she lied to her sister. Bree understood with complete certainty that she could no longer deny the facts.

She still had feelings for Patrick.

She had made a grievous error keeping his son from him. Though their relationship hadn't worked out, he would have been a good father.

The problem had been, still was, that he wanted to run everything. There was no compromise. He took his lawman tactics home. She hadn't been able to deal with that. Mutual respect was too important to her.

That wasn't fair. It wasn't that he hadn't respected her. He just hadn't wanted her doing anything he considered too dangerous for a woman…for his woman.

But none of that meant he wouldn't be a stellar father.

She had no idea what she was going to do.

Bree had spent nine years in law enforcement. She had solved the most puzzling cases, had apprehended her share of bad guys, including the worst of the worst—rapist and killers. And she had no idea how she was going to fix this.

Her life.

Her son's life.

How could she have ever hoped to keep Peter from knowing his father when they lived in the same county? Once Patrick moved from Monticello, Utah, to Kenner County she should have realized her mistake and corrected it then…before it went this far. She'd assumed at the time that if Patrick heard she'd had a child that he would probably believe Jack was the father.

"Truly dumb."

Bree should have anticipated the reality that babies grow up to be little boys and girls who ask questions. They then become teenagers who rebel against every per-ceived offense, real or imagined.

God, she was in trouble.

She took a breath, checked the time on her cell phone. She was also late.

Bree took a breath and walked out the door. If she stalled any longer she would be noticeably late. Nora would notice. Bree didn't want to offend Nora.

Dropping by her desk, she checked her messages before heading for lunch. She had no more excuses.

Making her way through Towaoc's one-level police station, a part of her kept hoping that the chief or one of her colleagues would call her name. If work got in the way, lunch would have to wait. Patrick could brief her by phone. She was fairly certain nothing new had come up on the Grainger case from his end any more than it had hers. Protocol dictated that all involved in the case get notification.

Before climbing into her borrowed SUV, she checked her cell phone once more.

She wasn't going to get a lucky break today.

En route to the Morning Ray Café, Bree replayed last night's close call. Patrick had shown up at her sister's demanding to know what was going on. Bree'd had to covertly call her sister and let her know to keep Peter inside. Not that she would have allowed him outside with what was going on. But Bree hadn't wanted to take any chances. Then Patrick had insisted on following her home, requiring Bree to ask her sister to drive Peter home as soon as Patrick was gone.

She owed her sister big-time.

The drive to Kenner City was spent worrying about facing Patrick after that kiss. Was it possible her sister had been right all along?

That kiss had certainly been…something. She'd melted like a bar of chocolate beneath the scorching desert sun. She shivered even now as she recalled the way his lips had felt pressed against hers. His big, strong hands cradling her face.

Bree had no idea Patrick had never married. That seemed impossible. A man who looked like him. A good, hardworking man.

With whom she'd argued vehemently

about her career. She'd been a green recruit assigned to the Ute Reservation when they'd first met. Patrick had been assigned to a special task force in Monticello. They'd worked a nasty hate-crime investigation in Utah territory together. Ended up head over heels in love and sharing an apartment for six months. But Patrick had rigid views on the differences between males and females in law enforcement, particularly the woman he loved. He didn't want her doing the dangerous details. The more intense the relationship had gotten the more protective he'd become.

Bree had felt smothered. She'd needed to be able to pursue her career as far as her abilities would take her. She'd wanted the tough cases, the danger. She hadn't wanted any more of Patrick's grief. So she'd walked. Two months later she'd discovered she was pregnant. Her cycles had never been regular. Missing one hadn't set off any alarms. But the second missed period had gotten her attention. No matter that they'd always practiced safe sex—she was pregnant. And Patrick hadn't come after her or even called in more than a month. Pride and vulnerability, along with her father's urging, had helped make her decision. *Move on.*

She'd been young and full of ambition. After Peter's birth and a hard-learned lesson in bad choices in husbands, she'd realized that risking her life was also risking her son's future. So she'd gone after the rank of detective. Even working homicide was a lot safer than pounding the pavement and cruising the alleyways and streets working in prevention mode.

Then, six years ago Patrick had come back home to Colorado to be sheriff of Kenner County and she'd sweated every single day of every damned year that he would somehow find out about her secret.

He'd called this morning to ensure she was okay, then insisted they needed to talk. Over lunch. God, how would she ever resolve this mess?

The drive down Main Street momentarily tugged Bree from her troubling thoughts. She loved this street. Kenner City was a grand old Western town without the overwhelming crowds of Park City. The refurbished storefronts made her think of the old Western movies she watched as a kid. From the well-maintained sidewalks to the majestic mountains in the distance, there was no place on the planet she'd rather be than here.

The Morning Ray Café sat on the corner of Main and Bridge Street. The perfect location for attracting tourists. But the locals were the mainstay of Nora's customers. Her decadent desserts and wide variety of home-cooked cuisine was known far and wide in these parts. Not to mention her vivacious personality. Everybody loved Nora.

The atmosphere was homey and warm and the diner was filled to capacity as always. From the working cowboys to the polished businessmen of the city's financial district, Nora got them all. The hum of conversation was underscored by the clink of silver and stoneware.

But it was the smell that had Bree's tummy rumbling. She had seriously missed this place. Savoring the delicious smells, she scanned the tables. Patrick sat in one of the only two booths in the diner. This one was near the back. The closest to the kitchen. Most patrons would avoid that booth, but not Patrick. Being close to the kitchen ensured his mother was able to visit with him even during a crowded lunch run like this one.

Patrick waved.

Bree's heart did one of those traitorous flip-flops. Dammit. She headed that way, weaving through the crowded tables.

He stood. Always the gentleman. His ever-present cowboy hat sat on the bench seat.

She'd missed that, too. There was a time when she'd loved to pull that hat off and run her fingers through his thick, dark hair.

Focus, Bree. Don't go there.

"Hey." It was the first word that popped into Bree's sluggish brain. Work. This was about work…not about the pale blue cotton shirt that stretched across his broad shoulders or the softly worn jeans that hugged his lean hips and long legs.

"Hey, yourself." He gestured to the booth. "I took the liberty of ordering for you."

Bree settled into her side of the booth working extra hard at not showing her surprise at the move. He used to do that all the time. It felt…too fast. Too much like old times.

"Okay," she said hesitantly.

"Mom's meat loaf." Patrick flashed her one of those lopsided grins that sent her heart bumping erratically. Peter smiled exactly like that.

He knew Nora's meatloaf was Bree's favorite.

Even she had to smile. "I do love Nora's meatloaf." She'd missed Nora and her amazing cooking. But coming here had been too risky…too painful.

Patrick slid into the booth and got down to business. "I hope you had better luck running down leads than I did this morning."

Nora's bubbly voice preceded her as she

burst through the double doors leading from the kitchen. She settled two glasses of water on the table.

"Bree, sugar, you are truly a sight for sore eyes."

Bree slid from the booth and accepted the hug Nora Martinez was all set to give. The buxom lady was barely five-four, but she made up for her height in personality and voice.

When Bree had settled back into her seat, Nora leaned down and kissed her son's head. "They never get too old or too big for that." She winked at Bree. "You'll find out one of these days."

Bree tensed.

"So, how have you been, sugar?" Nora braced a hip against the side of the booth.

"Good." That was true. "I made detective and I love my job." She thought of the homicide case she was working right now. "Most of the time, anyway."

"Well." Nora pushed away from the booth. "I'd better get hopping. You two enjoy."

Bree didn't realize how much she'd missed Nora until that moment. She had a way of making everything feel all right. She was definitely one of a kind.

Another reality hit Bree then. She had deprived Peter of knowing and loving his grandmother. A woman who would spoil her one and only grandchild to no end. Nora Martinez would be immensely disappointed in Bree for keeping Peter from her.

Bree's heart sank into her belly.

She had made a terrible mistake.

Stop. She had to stop obsessing about this. Whatever was going to happen would happen. She'd deal with the repercussions when it did.

Right now she had to focus.

"No luck with your contacts either?" she asked in answer to his question, steering the conversation to the reason they were here.

Patrick moved his head from side to side, his face grim. "I checked in with Ortiz a couple of hours ago. There's nothing new. They hope to have a preliminary autopsy report by tomorrow's briefing."

"Hopefully we'll learn something from the autopsy." Bree kept thinking about the ligature pattern on the victim's throat. Unusual but somehow familiar. She'd seen it somewhere.

"So," Patrick said, drawing her attention back to him, "how's married life?"

Surprise flared in her chest. Tension followed. Is that what he'd called her here to talk about? "I…I wouldn't know. I'm single."

His brow furrowed in that way that made Bree's heart skip a beat each time she saw Peter do the same thing. He'd never even met his father and yet he was so very much like him.

"I heard you'd gotten married," Patrick countered, not about to let it go.

"I did." She chose her words carefully. "Didn't work out so we divorced."

"When did that happen?"

"About a year ago." They'd been separated for six months before that but she wasn't going into the dirty details.

More of that surprise at just how wrong

he'd been flared in his eyes. He shrugged. "I guess I'm way behind on news."

Farther than you know.

"Any hits on the prints from your SUV?"

Something else she'd worked hard at keeping off her mind. "Not unless you count mine and my sister's and my..." She'd almost said her son. "My niece's." Too close.

"You wanna tell me about your anonymous fan?"

If she didn't he would just keep nagging at her. She'd kept the situation to herself until last night. Being a woman in the still predominantly man's world of law enforcement, any sign of weakness was looked upon in a different light. Since she hadn't had any real evidence someone was watching her, she'd let it go. But there was no letting it go now. This was real. She had a stalker. Filing an official report had been necessary.

She toyed with her water glass, mainly to avoid eye contact. "About two weeks ago I started to get this feeling that someone was watching me." She shrugged. "I'd get a glimpse of someone out of the corner of my eye. Notice the same vehicle mirroring my turns. You know. Stuff like that."

Nothing she could put her finger on, more gut instinct than anything.

"What about the phone calls?" Patrick asked.

Oh, yeah. She'd told him about that. "Several hang ups. Always from a public phone. No pattern as far as the time, but a definite pattern in the locations the calls were made from. Kenner City."

Patrick mulled over what she'd told him. "Have you made a list of anyone who might be holding a grudge? Someone you've ticked off in the line of duty or otherwise?"

Actually, her first instinct was to suspect Jack. But he'd left her alone for the past five or six months. She couldn't see any reason he would suddenly start trouble again now. They were beyond over. She'd seen him around with other women. Clearly he'd moved on.

"What about your ex?" Patrick asked, as if she'd spoken her thoughts.

Bree shook her head. "He's completely out of the picture." In fact, he'd actually been out of the picture all along. She just hadn't realized how much so.

Nora breezed through the kitchen doors. "Here we go, sweet things," she said happily. Her rosy cheeks, vivacious personality and bottled blond hair made her seem far younger than her nearly sixty years. She sat a steaming plate in front of Bree, then Patrick.

The presentation of the food was spectacular. Who knew that there could be such design significance in the way a plate of meat and two vegetables were laid out. Bree never ceased to be amazed at the way the lady could take something as simple as meatloaf and make it look beautiful. That it tasted magnificent as well didn't hurt. The smell was awesome.

Bree picked at her meatloaf. Time to turn the tables. To say at this point that she wasn't curious would be a vast understatement. A flat-out lie. "What about you? Is there a woman waiting at home?" She placed a piece of succulent meatloaf on her tongue. She had to fight the urge to moan.

Patrick picked up his fork and piddled with his food. "Not yet."

Aha. *Not yet.* Did that mean there was someone?

"I suppose you're like me," she suggested, deciding this was the best way out of this subject. She looked directly at him then. Ignored the ping of desire that hit deep beneath her belly button as those vivid blue eyes meshed with hers. "A little too busy for a decent social life?"

"Always." He poked a spoonful of mashed potatoes into his mouth.

She shouldn't have watched. He chewed, swallowed, then licked his lips. Her breath hitched.

Careful, Bree. This is dangerous territory. She was allowing herself to play with fire. Her sister should never have shown her that scrapbook. She hadn't been able to think about anything but what-if since.

She had to remember that any misstep she made now would impact her son.

Patrick had to remember that things hadn't worked out with Bree eight years ago. He could already see that their differences were still the same ones. She liked diving headfirst into intense investigations. Like murder. If he allowed himself to get involved with her again, his protective instincts would make them both miserable. He would only be unhappy.

That was no way to live.

The rest of the meal was eaten in silence, save for the occasional appearance of his mother. Nora had loved Bree. She'd wanted Patrick to settle down and make grandbabies for her.

Seeing them together now would only give her false hope. Patrick had chosen the diner because it represented a safe zone. But maybe he'd been wrong. The environment sure as hell hadn't done anything to slow his need to reach out and touch Bree. Or his burning desire to kiss her again.

Last night he'd dreamed of making love with her. The way they used to, with no inhibitions and with utter trust. At least until those last few weeks. Then the animosity had overridden everything else.

As much as he wanted to stay and learn all he could about her life the past eight years, he had a three o'clock appointment. They'd discussed what little they could do on the Grainger case until the next briefing or until they picked up an additional lead. Trawling for info was about the extent of it. The truth was, sitting here looking at her was pure torture. He needed distance. His upcoming appointment was a blessing.

Before he could voice his need to get back to the office, Bree pushed her coffee cup aside. They'd both declined dessert but no one could pass on his mother's coffee. Her own special blend drew folks from far and wide for a cup of Nora's Good Morning Coffee.

"I have a staff meeting. I need to get

back." She glanced at the long counter lined with customers, then toward the kitchen doors. "I should get my check and…go."

"You're kidding, right?" Patrick finished off his coffee, then set his cup aside. "You know Nora's not going to let you pay."

Bree scooted from the booth. "Thank her for me, would you?"

The kitchen's swinging doors flew open and Nora Martinez scurried out. Patrick glanced at Bree as he got to his feet. "I guess we'll both get the chance to thank her."

Nora urged Bree to come again soon, then hugged her twice. Clearly Patrick wasn't the only one who still had feelings for Bree.

Crossing the dining room, Patrick hesitated. Ben Parrish was deep in conversation with a woman. Patrick studied his body language a moment. The two seemed to be arguing or at the very least having an intense exchange. The wavy red hair triggered recognition. Ava Wright, one of the forensic techs at the crime lab. Interesting. The idea that Parrish was currently a person of interest in the Grainger investigation made the fact that the two were having such a tense lunch only a step or two away from suspicious.

"Isn't that Agent Parrish?" Bree asked.

"It is." Patrick opted not to jump to conclusions. He cut through the tables and pushed out the door.

"I'll see you at the briefing tomorrow," Bree said, already moving away from him.

"Just one more thing." He should have done this first. She turned back to him, those wide brown eyes expectant. He rotated his hat in his hands. "I want to apologize again for last night. Like I said, that won't happen again. I don't see why we can't be friends despite the past. Who knows? This may not be the only time we end up working together. It's best that we do this the right way." Okay. Whew. He'd gotten the entire speech out without screwing up.

Bree studied him for two beats, just long enough for him to start to sweat. "You're right. Friends is…good. We should work at that."

Patrick's chest expanded with a deep, relieved breath. "Good."

She glanced at her borrowed SUV. "Gotta go."

Patrick settled his hat into place. "Keep me posted on this stalker business," he urged.

She didn't make any promises. He watched as she moved toward the driver's-side door of an SUV marked with the Towaoc PD logo.

Patrick didn't get into his SUV until he'd watched her drive away. His instincts were humming. What was she not telling him? Was there more to this stalker business than she'd let on?

He didn't like the idea that she was taking this so cavalierly. The warning left on her SUV was clear and to the point.

Someone was obviously watching her.

Someone who wanted to scare her…or worse.

AFTER HER STAFF MEETING Bree headed for the parking lot. She called Tabitha as she climbed into the truck to let her know she would be picking up her son from school. Once this investigation heated up, who knew when she'd have the opportunity to pick him up again.

The press was already badgering anyone they discovered was involved with the investigation. Ortiz planned to hold a news conference after the briefing tomorrow to ease the speculation.

The hounding for information would only get worse after that.

"How did your day go, son?" she asked Peter as he climbed in.

He dropped his backpack onto the floorboard and stretched his safety belt into place. "It wasn't so good." Those big blue eyes, heavy with frustration, peered up at her. "Robby Benson told me my daddy must be dead since I've never seen him. Is that true, Mommy? Is my daddy dead?"

Bree slipped her foot from the brake to the accelerator and rolled out of the pickup lane. Why did kids have to be so cruel?

Why did adults have to lie?

She was no better than Robby Benson. She couldn't keep avoiding the subject and she refused to outright lie to her son about his father. He'd never asked where he was or who he was. He'd never asked much of anything, until recently. Turning seven a couple of months ago had changed everything. "Your daddy doesn't live with us" didn't cut it anymore.

"No, baby, your father is not dead." Did she say he lived far away…that he was too busy? That had worked in the past.

Peter pondered that answer for a moment. Bree braced for what no doubt came next.

"Then why doesn't he ever come to see me? Robby's daddy just bought him the coolest bike ever. Has my daddy ever bought me anything?"

And so it began in earnest.

Just how was she going to do this? She'd already chosen a path…one that was about to bite her in the butt. "Well, sweetie, it's—"

A dark sedan with equally dark windows

made the next turn Bree executed. Her instincts went immediately on point. "Hold on a minute, son."

Okay, so that was just one turn…that she'd noted, anyway. No need to get paranoid just yet. She made another turn, this one unnecessary, just to see if the sedan would follow.

That was an affirmative. Her pulse rate jumped into overdrive.

She glanced at her son. Couldn't risk going cowboy and confronting the driver of the vehicle. If she made any overt moves of aggression her son's life could be put in danger.

The car suddenly lurched forward, got as close to her rear bumper as possible without nudging her.

Her breath caught.

She was barely out of town. She could turn around.

"Lean back hard against your seat, baby." God, if this guy hit her…

The car jerked left, roared forward. She

eased closer to the side of the road, let off the accelerator.

The sedan rocketed past her. She squinted, tried to see the license plate but the car was too fast and she was too rattled. If her son hadn't been in the vehicle with her she would have given pursuit.

She could call it in, but she didn't have a handle on the make and model or the license plate number.

But she and Peter were okay and that was what mattered.

Relief struck with such force that her fingers barely managed to keep a grip on the steering wheel as she picked up speed once more.

Calm down. It was over now.

Now she knew one thing for sure. This wasn't going away and it was no teenage prank.

This latest incident was no coincidence. And it damned sure wasn't her imagination.

Someone was following her…watching her.

He wasn't going to stop until he'd accomplished his goal.

To scare her?

Or to kill her?

Chapter Six

Bree arrived at the annex building for the Wednesday afternoon briefing with five minutes to spare. She'd gotten through last night without more questions from her son. Sheer luck. One of his friends from school had needed to sleep over since his mother had gone into labor with her second child.

Bree understood that her luck wouldn't hold out.

The one question Peter had asked was when would he have a little brother or sister.

Now there was a question she sure couldn't answer.

She sat in the borrowed TPD SUV and wondered for the umpteenth time what she was going to do. Last night's tossing and turning had left her sleep deprived and frustrated with herself. And her dreams. She'd dreamed of Patrick…and the way things used to be. Before all the tension and yelling.

"Enough." She had to focus on this case. Dealing with her personal life would just have to come later. If she were really lucky, a lot later.

Now her stalker…that was something she might just have to deal with sooner than later.

He—assuming it was a he—knew where she lived. Where her son went to school. She'd spoken to Peter's teacher last night and warned her that there was a potential problem. Bree had also spoken with her chief. Two of her colleagues had spent the morning going over her case files for the past couple of years. They'd found nothing that appeared motive enough to prompt retribution.

Until she had more to go on she'd just have to wait it out. That was the thing with stalkers. There was nothing the victim could do until the perp was caught in the act of wrongdoing or had left evidence of his illegal act. There was certainly nothing to be done when the stalker's identity was unknown.

Unfortunately Bree was trapped in that freaky zone where she could do nothing but be aware and be patient. Hope for the best and brace for the worst.

A car parked a couple of spaces over and Ortiz emerged. When he'd gone inside she climbed out and headed that way as well. She didn't see Patrick's SUV. Maybe he was hung up with something else. Had to be something big for him to miss this briefing. He would likely send one of his deputies to cover for him.

Bree took the stairs to the third floor, waved in greeting to the receptionist and for identification purposes, then moved on to the command center. The room was crowded with federal agents already.

Bree took the only available seat and smiled when Callie MacBride looked her way. Callie's return smile was weary. She wore that strained look again. The one that said this case was getting to her. Bree wondered again if she and the victim had been particularly close. There was definitely some aspect of this investigation that was getting to her on a level she couldn't contain. Murder was bad any way you looked at it, but Bree had seen the lady in action before and Callie was as tough as nails. This wasn't her typical reaction.

The scrape of a chair being dragged up next to her drew her attention back to the here and now. Patrick settled into the seat.

Bree's heart reacted instantly with a thump then a stumble. She looked away. Drew in a deep breath.

As if her racing heart wasn't bad enough, her body temperature climbed a few degrees.

Maybe if she hadn't deprived herself of male company for the past eighteen months she wouldn't be so needy.

That had to be the explanation for her reactions to his presence. That or her body was mistaking fear for desire.

She wasn't sure which was worse, being scared to death he would discover her secret or harboring forbidden desire for the man with whom she had a rocky past. Either one was treacherous territory.

"You okay?" Patrick asked for her ears only. The sincere concern in his eyes drew her like a magnet. He'd always been able to do that. To make her want him with just a look.

Bree wished Ortiz would call the briefing to order. Most of the agents were still milling around, talking among themselves…except for Callie and Ben Parrish. Both had already taken their seats and appeared lost in their own thoughts.

"I'm fine." Bree pulled her notepad from her jacket pocket and placed it on the table in preparation for the start of the briefing. Mainly she did it to prevent having to meet Patrick's gaze again. That didn't stop him from watching her. She could feel his eyes probing her, looking for the crack that would let him in.

"Any more trouble with whoever sent you that warning?" He pulled his chair an inch or two closer.

Her pulse raced.

Her first instinct was to tell him no. But he would read the lie in her posture and on her face. He was too good at reading body language to miss the slightest hint of deception.

"There was a car yesterday," she began, but got distracted by Elizabeth Reddawn hovering at the door. She waved to someone in the room, a large brown envelope in her hand.

Bree scanned the crowd, which was still caught up in conversation. Ben Parrish pointed to his chest and the receptionist nodded. He pushed back his chair and moved wide around the other agents to reach the door. Elizabeth passed him the envelope and hurried back to the lobby to man her desk.

Parrish stared at the envelope for a long moment, glanced back at the other agents, then rushed into the corridor.

"Wonder what that was about?" Patrick whispered to her.

She shivered, hoped like hell he didn't see it. "Don't know."

"I spoke to Ortiz earlier today," Patrick said quietly. "He explained that Parrish, Ryan, Dylan Acevedo and Grainger all attended the Bureau academy together. They've been close friends ever since, despite being assigned to different field offices." Patrick surveyed the assembled group. "There are a lot of intense emotions tangled up in this bunch."

That cleared up a number of questions for Bree. In her experience with federal agents, rigid professionalism were the buzzwords. But this case was, as she suspected, deeply personal.

"You were saying something about a car?" Patrick asked.

Bree had hoped he'd forgotten about that. "I picked up…" Bree froze. She almost said she'd picked her son up from school. This was the second time she'd had a close call like this. She had to pull it together. "I picked up milk on my way home yesterday afternoon." That was true.

She had stopped at the Stop and Go. "Anyway, a dark sedan, one with heavily tinted windows, roared up behind me and stayed on my bumper for a bit before barreling around me. It might not have been related." She thought about those moments when she feared the sedan would ram the SUV she was driving. "It felt like an intimidation tactic." She shrugged. "But I was in the TPD vehicle. It could have been someone who just doesn't like cops."

"Bree."

She didn't want to look at him. It was easier to watch the other folks in the room.

"Bree," he said more firmly.

Reluctantly, she met his gaze.

"You have to take this situation seriously. Talk to your chief."

"I already have." God, she needed a distraction here. Anything to move the moment beyond this discussion.

On cue, and much to her relief, Ben Parrish reentered the room. He no longer clutched the envelope the receptionist had given him but judging by the grim expression he wore, whatever had been in that envelope was not good news.

Like her, Patrick watched Parrish take his seat. Bree wished she could read his mind. Obviously he was brutally torn. Was there something he'd done that made him feel somehow responsible for Grainger's death? Bree still didn't believe he was the murderer. She doubted anyone in this room really believed that. But Parrish felt guilty about something. That much was apparent.

"What did your chief say?" Patrick wanted to know.

She didn't want to talk about this with him. She knew to be aware. For now, that was all she could do. Thankfully, before she was forced to respond, Ortiz called the room to order.

Ortiz briefly reviewed their findings thus far, which were pretty much nil. No match had been found for the ligature pattern on the victim's throat. However, the coroner had determined that the item used to strangle Agent Grainger was metal. Silver. The unknown subject, perpetrator in regular cop speak, was suspected to be male due to the depth of the marks. Massive strength had been utilized.

Bree's chest tightened at the idea that Agent Grainger, although highly trained, hadn't had a chance against such raw brawn.

Acevedo pushed away from the table and walked over to the only window in the room to stare at the mountains in the distance. Ryan exchanged a tense look with Parrish. Ortiz paused only a moment, probably to ensure another physical confrontation wasn't going to break out, before continuing the briefing.

While Ortiz reviewed the details he intended to pass along to the press, Bree watched the people in the room. Acevedo lingered at the window and Parrish remained at the table with his head hung as if in defeat. More tension-filled glances were exchanged, these between Ryan and Callie.

Bree wondered if there was something far more personal than friendship between those two. Then again, she could be reading too much into the turbulent emotions of those involved in this investigation.

Acevedo returned to his seat and he and Ryan spoke quietly. Ryan appeared to be attempting to persuade the other agent to stay calm. Parrish cut a look at his two friends then dropped his head once more.

Again, Bree couldn't help feeling sorry for him. Yes, he'd found the body. Yes, he was male and clearly capable of the necessary strength to strangle the victim in the manner the coroner described. But why not make a run for it? Why keep coming back to face this hostility?

It couldn't be as simple as him being the killer.

Agent Tom Ryan passed out copies of a recent photo of Julie Grainger to all involved with the investigation. Ortiz suggested that local law enforcement continue to prod their contacts. The Bureau remained focused on the Del Gardo connection. Since there was no evidence to indicate otherwise, and likely for other reasons not shared, they were convinced at

this point Del Gardo or someone in his or-
ganization had something to do with her
murder. As he reiterated this conclusion,
Ryan and Acevedo stared pointedly at
Parrish.

Did his fellow agents believe Parrish
was somehow involved with Del Gardo or
his activities? If so, no one was saying as
much out loud. At least not with Bree and
Patrick present.

That would make Parrish a traitor…
whether he was a killer or not.

Ortiz had just dismissed the meeting
when Bree's cell phone vibrated. She
checked the screen. Officer Cyrus. Bree
quickly stepped into the corridor to take
the call. Maybe he had found something
that would determine who was stalking
her.

"Hunter."

"Detective, this is Steve Cyrus."

"You have news for me, Cyrus?" It
would be damned nice to solve the case of
her mystery stalker. She would feel a lot
better about her son's safety.

"Yes, ma'am. I got a call from one of the drunks I pick up on a regular basis. He likes building up brownie points so I'll go easy on him when he's on a drinking binge."

Bree understood that strategy. Leverage was a good thing when dealing with informants with criminal tendencies, however minor.

"This guy swears he saw someone matching Sherman Watts's description arguing with Agent Grainger not more than a week ago. He was afraid to ask Sherman if it was him, but he's certain it was."

Sherman Watts? Watts was a local troublemaker. To Bree's knowledge he'd never murdered anyone. Most of his rap sheet consisted of drunk and disorderly charges. He could be a pain in the butt, but so far as she knew he wasn't a killer.

Some part of her was disappointed that the news wasn't related to the jerk who had spray painted her SUV.

But it was about the Grainger case.

"How reliable is this informant?"

Adrenaline whipped across Bree's nerve endings. This could in some small way be their first real break.

"He's never failed me before. The best I can tell, he and Watts are occasional drinking buddies. What he saw might mean nothing at all, but I thought it would be worth checking out."

"Thanks, Cyrus." The need to end the call and hunt down Watts charged through her veins. "We're looking at any and all leads. This could give us a definite starting place. I'll talk to Watts and see what he has to say." If she could find him. He had a way of making himself scarce when he was avoiding the law. Which was rather frequently. She mentally ticked off a list of places to start looking, none of them on the Chamber of Commerce's lists of places to visit when in Four Corners.

"I wouldn't go looking for him alone," Cyrus cautioned. "If he's involved in this he might be more desperate than usual."

Bree told herself his warning had nothing to do with her being a woman and everything to do with taking the necessary precautions despite the urgency of the situation. Two days around Patrick and she was already defensive about her physical limitations.

Like Julie Grainger must have felt during those final moments of her life. A shudder rocked Bree. No matter one's training, the element of surprise when combined with lethal intent was a damned near insurmountable opponent. A deadly opponent.

Bree thanked Cyrus and slid her phone back into its holster. At least she had a lead to follow. A starting place. Knowing Watts's penchant for womanizing it could be a dead end. The incident might be as simple as Watts making a remark or hitting on Grainger and Grainger dressing him down in public.

"Ortiz is holding a press conference in one hour."

Startled, Bree turned to face Patrick. She schooled her expression in the hopes of keeping her reactions to herself. Hearing his voice again was just something she hadn't gotten used to yet. Having heard it in her dreams far too many times didn't count. Nor had it been necessary to remind her of the way it wrapped around her and made her want to lean into him. Every nuance was permanently imprinted in her memory. The rich, deep timbre was another of those things she had struggled so diligently, without success, to forget.

"The press conference. Right." She nodded, still a little distracted by Cyrus's call. And the mere sound of Patrick's voice.

"Ortiz is heading back to Durango after that," he continued, seemingly without realizing how he'd affected her. "He'll be staying on top of the investigation via teleconference unless he's needed back here. Tom Ryan is in charge of the investigation now."

Focus. She had to find Watts. But Cyrus was right. She didn't need to go it alone. "I…may have a lead." She and Patrick were supposed to be working together on this. A team. Telling him, taking him along were the right things to do.

"Is that what your call was about?"

Oh, yeah, he was watching her every move. "It was. According to one of Officer Cyrus's contacts, Agent Grainger had a confrontation with Sherman Watts only a couple of days before she was murdered. Considering Watts's obnoxious personality and lecherous ways the confrontation may have been happenstance, but I figure it's worth checking out."

Patrick was familiar with Watts. His wasn't a name Patrick had expected to hear connected with Agent Grainger's murder, but men like Watts were fully capable of the unexpected.

"I was thinking," Bree suggested, "that we should track Watts down and shake him up a little. Get the truth out of him. He runs in some low circles. Even if there's nothing to his confrontation with Grainger, he might know something."

Most of the agents were filtering out of the command center now. There was no reason for the two of them to hang around any longer. Patrick nodded. "Let's do it."

He gestured for her to precede him. "I'll drive."

"Fine by me," she tossed over her shoulder as she joined the exodus.

Maybe having her go first wasn't such a good idea, but it was the gentlemanly thing to do. Even if the sway of her slender hips distracted him in a wholly unprofessional way.

They'd made a deal. Friends. Colleagues.

Damn, but that was going to be a hard bargain to keep.

FINDING SHERMAN WATTS wasn't an easy task. Patrick drove to every unsavory hangout he and Bree could think of. It wasn't until they hit the casino in Towaoc that they found a clue as to his whereabouts. One of Patrick's repeat offenders, one with sticky fingers, was happy to report that Watts had been hanging out at a friend's in a trailer park outside the city limits of Towaoc.

"Not exactly uptown," Bree commented, taking in the unsightly conditions of the trailer park as they arrived at the address given.

"Not exactly," Patrick agreed.

The grounds were littered with trash. Most of the vehicles parked next to the dilapidated trailers were equally dilapidated. Music blared through the thin walls of the one closest to the park entrance.

"We're looking for lot ten." Patrick searched the ends of the narrow tin-can homes for the lot numbers. Some were worn nearly beyond the point of legibility. Others were missing entirely.

"Should be the next one on the right." Bree pointed to a rusty box with a broken-down deck leading to its front door.

"His friend must be doing pretty well," Patrick said, noting the new-looking truck parked in the dirt drive. "Too bad it's likely something illegal."

Bree called in the license plate number. The more information at their disposal, the more power and leverage they possessed.

Patrick emerged from his SUV slowly,

scanning the area. There was no way to guess what you could run upon in a dump like this. Better safe than sorry. He rested his hand on the butt of his revolver. Bree did the same.

Patrick climbed the steps of the deck first. Bree hung back to answer her cell. Patrick listened for any sound coming from inside the trailer. Nothing. He stepped to the side of the door, opted not to draw his weapon just yet, then he pounded on the metal door with his fist.

"Sherman Watts, this is Sheriff Martinez. I need to have a word with you."

Bree moved into position on the other side of the door. She drew her weapon and assumed an offense ready stance.

No movement inside.

Patrick pounded harder. "Sherman Watts!"

A bump then a crash inside warned Patrick that someone was up and moving about. He braced. The door swung open, concealing Bree behind it.

"What the hell do you want, Sheriff?"

Watts, half-dressed and looking like he had one hell of a hangover, swayed in the open doorway. His long, stringy hair didn't look as if it had been washed in a month. Those beady eyes, red from alcohol abuse, glared at Patrick.

The man wasn't armed. Patrick hadn't actually expected him to be, unless he was concealing a weapon in his baggy jeans.

"I need to ask you a few questions. May we come in?"

Watts looked around. "Who's we?"

Bree stepped from behind the door, her weapon holstered now. "Evening, Sherman." She looked the middle-aged man up and down. "Looks like you've been doing a little better at the poker table." She hitched her head toward the truck. "That's a very nice truck you bought last week."

Patrick met her gaze. The vehicle did belong to Watts. A big move up from the rusty old truck he'd been driving for years. If he'd only just registered it last week, then that meant he'd come into some fast money.

Could it be blood money?

"Maybe," Patrick said to Watts, drawing his attention back to him, "you'll share some of your winning secrets with us."

Watts scoffed. "I don't have no secrets." He folded his arms over his skinny chest. "I won that truck fair and square in a private game of chance." He smirked. "I could give you the names of the fellers I beat, but they'd probably just lie and say they was the ones who won. I don't see where it's any of your business anyway."

"We're not here about the truck," Bree told him.

His smirk faded. "What the hell you want then?"

"May we come in?" Patrick repeated.

Watts allowed his gaze to skim Bree's body. "Why not? I like cops." He said the last with a lecherous grin. "Ain't my place anyhow."

Patrick shouldered him out of the way as he moved through the door. "I'm a cop. You like me?"

Watts backed up a couple of steps. "Don't

get your boxers in a wad, Sheriff. I just woke up. I'm not my usual pleasant self yet."

"It's almost six p.m.," Bree informed him as she stepped inside. "What's wrong, Watts? You aren't sleeping well at night?"

He flicked those beady eyes in her direction. "I never sleep at night. Too much happening at night. You know what I mean?" He sniggered.

"Speaking of happenings," Patrick interjected. "Did you hear about the federal agent who was murdered?"

Watts tensed. Only the slightest shift in his posture, but Patrick didn't miss it.

"I don't listen to the news."

Patrick surveyed the trailer's front room. Ragged furniture. Looked like the place had been tossed but he knew that Watts and his friend were probably just slobs. They would live here until it became completely unbearable and then they'd move to the next dump.

"Julie Grainger." Bree pulled the photo from her jacket pocket. She shoved it in Watts's face. "I understand you knew her."

Watts reared his head back and studied the photo for all of three seconds. "She's a looker. I wish I'd known her."

"The way I heard it—" Patrick walked around the room as if looking for contraband "—the two of you had quite a public disagreement."

Watts followed Patrick's every move, his guard fully in place now. "Well, you heard wrong. If I'd known that bitch, we wouldn't've been arguing."

Bree went toe-to-toe with Watts. "I think maybe you wanted to know her and she took one look at your ugly mug and told you to get lost."

Patrick's pulse skipped. What was she doing getting in this bastard's face like that?

Watts snickered. "Nah, lady cop, you got the wrong man. I don't know nothing about your dead friend. I never seen her before."

Patrick pushed his way between the two. "Why don't we have you come in for questioning just the same," Patrick suggested. "We're just trying to be thorough with our investigation. You know, follow all the leads whether they pan out or not."

Watts searched Patrick's eyes, didn't so much as blink as he met the challenge there. "Name the time and place, Sheriff, and I'll be there."

"I may do that sooner than you think," Patrick countered. "You're a person of interest in this case, Watts. Be sure you're available. I'm certain we'll be talking again very soon."

"You know where to look for me," Watts called as they walked out the door. "Send your pretty squaw on over any time."

Patrick stopped dead in his tracks. For two beats the only thing he could see was rage red. The need to pound Watts into an unrecognizable pulp was a palpable force inside him. It took every ounce of strength he possessed not to turn around and beat the hell out of the guy with his bare hands.

Bree didn't wait. She stamped back to the SUV and climbed in.

Patrick took a deep breath and didn't look back. Getting himself slapped with an assault charge wouldn't help this investigation. But he was sure itching to punch the bastard. Patrick opened the driver's-side door and settled behind the wheel of his SUV. Watts stared directly at Patrick one last time before smirking, then slamming his door shut.

Bastard.

When Patrick had guided his SUV back onto the highway and the trailer park was in the rearview mirror, Bree turned to him.

He'd expected this. He'd opened his mouth prematurely back there. But he was right whether she wanted to hear it or not.

"I don't need you playing the protector when we're interviewing a possible suspect. I had the situation with Watts under control."

She spoke calmly and quietly but the underlying fury in her voice told him she was mad as hell.

"You shouldn't have pushed your luck. You got right in the man's face, Bree. That's a dangerous maneuver if you can't back it up."

Wrong thing to say. Again.

"I can't believe you!" She glared at the highway in front of them. "I'm every bit as well trained as you. I can handle myself. I know how far to go with an interrogation. And it wasn't like I didn't have backup available."

He could argue with her but that would only make bad matters worse. "You're right. I'm wrong. Let's not argue." He told himself that he could see her side, but he didn't. Not really. Was he wrong? "Okay?"

His halfhearted apology didn't help.

She fumed silently, wouldn't give him a response.

"We see things differently on that point," he offered. "My concern is not an indication of any lack of faith in your ability."

No comment.

Perfect.

Fine. Focus on the investigation. Let her fume. "I'll pass along what we learned about Watts to Agent Ortiz. See if he wants us to follow up with surveillance or additional questioning." The suggestion immediately produced images of him and Bree stuck inside this SUV all night long…in the dark.

More silence.

Great. "What do you want me to say, Bree?" This was just like eight years ago.

"Nothing. You've already said all I needed to hear. Nothing's changed."

And that was what he got for caring.

Chapter Seven

The next morning Bree parked, turned off the engine and stared out at the barren landscape that was the last sight Julie Grainger had laid eyes on before being murdered.

According to the coroner Julie had been dead approximately forty-eight to fifty hours when her body was discovered.

That meant she had possibly died about this time of morning, eight or nine. Five days ago.

Less than a week.

Bree got out of her truck and closed the door. The sound echoed, reminding her she was alone. No work. No family. No Patrick.

She needed to think.

Hand on the butt of her weapon, she walked slowly toward the yellow tape that marked the perimeter of the crime scene. It drooped here and there, a sign of the passage of time.

With no real break in the case.

They were beyond that crucial forty-eight-hour mark. And they had nothing significant to show for it.

Patrick had discussed the Sherman Watts situation with Agent Ortiz. His people were going to take over the follow-up. The press conference hadn't garnered any reaction as far as Bree had heard. Oritz had been brief and to the point. He'd urged anyone with information to come forward. There wasn't really a lot Bree could do at this point except react to new leads, those called in or the ones she drummed up pounding the pavement and rattling the cages of informants.

Bree stopped before reaching the yellow tape. She crouched down and picked up a handful of the sandy dirt. She rubbed it between her fingers, let it drift back to the ground. What was Julie doing out here so early on a Saturday morning?

Had one of her contacts in the Del Gardo investigation asked to meet her in this barren place? Or was her killer someone she'd rubbed the wrong way in a previous investigation? Or just some lowlife who had nothing to do with any of her cases.

In law enforcement there was always that chance. Many times the family of someone you'd helped convict would seek vengeance. Or you'd find yourself at the wrong place at the wrong time.

Had Sherman Watts met Julie here? Was the drunken weasel capable of killing? More significant, was he smart enough, quick enough to catch her by surprise and overpower her physically?

Bree blinked away the images her thoughts evoked. Slowly, she turned all the way around and surveyed the vast land-scape. Rugged and barren, but beautiful in its own right.

Her own life felt a little like that sometimes. She'd had her heart broken, her pride battered and her social skills had taken a hiatus. But she had her beautiful son.

Unlike Julie Grainger, Bree was alive. As long as she was alive there was hope for change…for better things. For smarter decisions.

What, Bree wondered, would Julie have done differently if she'd known her life would end so suddenly? Were there things left she needed or wanted to say? Decisions she would have made differently?

Bree would spend more time with her son for sure.

She thought of Peter's excitement about today's field trip when she'd dropped him off at school this morning. For the moment he'd forgotten all about asking questions about his father.

Bree was relieved, but she knew that wasn't fair. She couldn't carry on this lie much longer. The guilt was gnawing at her.

But then, at times like yesterday's visit with Sherman Watts, she wanted to punch

Patrick. They were no longer involved. Hadn't spoken until three days ago in nearly eight years. How could he step into her professional space and treat her as if she were incapable? As if she was still that young, green rookie?

But that was exactly what he had done then and he was doing it again now. That whole macho cowboy thing was driving her crazy.

At least when he wasn't making her wish she'd made different choices. His voice…those eyes…just being near him made her want to reach out and touch him. To be kissed by him.

Again.

And again.

She closed her eyes and dropped her head back. She had tried so hard for so long to pretend she didn't care about him. He damn sure hadn't tried to get her back. Hadn't even called. Her father had insisted that was all the proof Bree needed that Patrick didn't care and certainly didn't deserve her. She belonged with her people.

She should make her and her child's life here…where they belonged. She allowed her father to do exactly what she'd sworn she would never permit.

She'd pushed on with her career. She'd stayed busy raising her son. And she'd even allowed herself to get married.

Big fat mistake.

But she'd gone for it.

Seeing Patrick again. Being with his mother even if only for a brief lunch reminded Bree of all she'd walked away from. Of all she'd deprived her son of having. Not once had Bree considered how her decision would impact Nora, Patrick's only family. Or Peter, for that matter, where a paternal grandparent was concerned. He had a whole other family and she had kept him from that part of *his* life. But she'd been so young, so scared.

She couldn't keep pretending that life would go back to the way it was. Pretending Patrick didn't exist or matter was no longer feasible. She simply couldn't do it any longer.

He'd kissed her. He still had feelings for her just as her sister had said. But any feelings he had left would vanish the instant he learned how she had deceived him. He would hate her.

This was no little thing.

"Oh, by the way, Patrick, you have a son?" His age? "Oh, he's seven years old."

Bree groaned.

This was going to be bad.

Peter would be thrilled to have a father. That he was a sheriff would give him that superhero persona he longed for in a male authority figure.

No—in a father. That was what Peter wanted more than anything. A father.

His father.

"Not good. Not good."

Bree scanned the cliff dwelling and the mountains in the distance one last time. There was an emptiness here that mirrored her emotions. She had to find a way to fill that gaping hole.

For her son.

For her.

But what would she lose in the process?

"Just go to work, Bree." There was nothing she could do about any of it this morning.

She trudged back to the SUV. Borrowing trouble wasn't her style. Taking this one step at a time was the key. Talk to her sister. Talk to Peter. Then present the facts to Patrick.

Logical. Rational. Just like her police work. Analyze the situation, present the facts, form a conclusion and take action.

Simple.

"Right."

She reached for the driver's-side door of the SUV and the hair on the back of her neck lifted.

Bree whirled around, her hand instinctively resettled on the butt of her weapon. Her heart rate rushed into rapid fire. She searched the terrain, looking for whatever had set her instincts on point.

She hadn't felt that creepy "being watched" sensation since the day before yesterday. But that sensation was exactly what she was experiencing right now.

As if someone was hiding out there, watching her…waiting for the right moment.

For what?

To do to her what someone had done to Julie Grainger?

The thumping in her chest sped up.

By God, she wasn't going to make it easy.

She checked the interior of the SUV since she hadn't locked it, then climbed in. Keeping an eye on her surroundings, she started the engine and did a one-eighty turnabout.

For the first time in her career she wondered if Patrick was right. Maybe she did take too many chances while ignoring the danger. Otherwise she wouldn't be out here in the middle of nowhere alone knowing that someone was watching her.

It was real. She knew it was. Her vandalized SUV proved that. The car that threatened her with its aggressive driving could have been coincidence.

But not the vandalism.

Yet, she didn't listen.

She pretended the threat didn't exist.

The same way she'd pretended Patrick didn't for all these years.

And now that was coming back to haunt her. How long before her determination to prove she wasn't afraid of any kind of challenge also came back to haunt her?

Five o'clock.

Patrick stared at his phone. He hadn't called Bree today. She damned sure hadn't called him. He'd been playing catch-up all day at the office. Running a sheriff's department wasn't a duty that could be ignored. It was a constant balancing act between the police work and the political side of the job.

The political side was something he could live without but it went with the territory.

His personal life…that was something he'd ignored far too long.

Spending time with Bree again made him all too aware of that seriously neglected aspect of his life.

How in hell could they get along if she was going to be so haphazard with her safety? He couldn't pretend not to be aware of the risks she took. She was in law enforcement. Danger went with the territory.

Why couldn't she understand that he wasn't attempting to control her life? He was trying to protect her.

Because he cared.

Far more deeply than he wanted to admit.

But he wasn't so sure she felt the same way. He'd noticed tiny reactions when they were together. But not the kind of reactions he felt whenever she was near. Not that he could see, anyway.

If, *major* if, she still had feelings for him, maybe they could start over. Begin back at square one and get to know each other all over again. They could adjust. He could try harder not to smother her.

That was what she had accused him of. She'd sworn that no man would ever control her life the way her father, although she loved him, had controlled her mother's. And he'd done nothing. Just let her walk away. For the first four of five months he'd been certain she would come back. But she hadn't. Then he'd convinced himself it was too late. After that it had been easier not to look back.

Was that why she was single again? Had her husband attempted too much control?

Patrick had never met a woman with a more determined spirit than Bree. Well, maybe his mother was a close match. She'd certainly never allowed a man to control her life, not even Patrick. His father had passed away when he was a kid and his mother had been making it on her own ever since.

But he didn't want Bree to be alone the way his mother was. He'd watched when Nora thought he wasn't looking and he recognized the loneliness.

Truth was, he didn't want to end up alone either. Time had already proven that he was a one-woman man. No one else had made him feel the way Bree did. He'd even worked hard at a short-term relationship or two. But he just hadn't experienced that magic with anyone else. He was approaching forty. The time to change course was running short.

Only one way to fix this.

He picked up the phone and called Bree's cell. The worst she could do was say no.

She answered and for a moment he couldn't speak. He didn't want her to say no.

"Hello? Patrick?"

She'd recognized his number on her caller ID. "Bree." Suck it up, buddy. "I think it's time we cleared up a few things." Too damned demanding. "I mean… mended some fences." Take a breath. "If you're not busy I'd like to take you to dinner tonight. I mean…if you're available. You do have to eat."

Lame, Patrick. Damned lame.

The silence on the other end of the line had his gut in knots.

"Okay."

Relief surged through him. "Great. So I'll pick you up at seven?"

"Seven," she agreed.

When they'd said their goodbyes, Patrick closed his cell and leaned back in his chair.

He blew out a big, relieved breath.

"Sheriff?"

Patrick's head came up. His assistant loitered in the door. "Yeah, Clayton?"

"I have some information you might find useful."

Confusion furrowed Patrick's brow. He motioned for his assistant to come on in and have a seat. "What sort of information?"

Clayton closed the door behind him, crossed the room and took a seat in front of Patrick's desk. "About Detective Hunter."

Well, hell. How long had the man been standing there listening? When Patrick shot him an accusatory look his assistant seemed to get the point.

"Yes," Clayton admitted, "I overheard your phone call."

When Patrick would have dressed him down for eavesdropping, Clayton held up a hand and insisted, "Hear me out."

At this point, what did Patrick have to lose? His assistant was already eyeball-deep in his personal business.

"I was talking to the receptionist over at TPD."

Great, now the world would know. Patrick rolled his eyes.

"About a report we need from one of their robbery detectives," Clayton said, evidently reading Patrick's mind.

Patrick motioned for him to get on with it.

"Well, according to Mary Jane, the receptionist," he clarified, "Bree's ex-husband was a real piece of work. A total scumbag."

"Explain," Patrick ordered, tension radiating with rapid fire speed.

"His name is Jackson Raintree. He's a bully, a heavy drinker and, again, according to Mary Jane, he roughed Bree up a couple of times during the final days of their relationship."

Patrick sat up straighter. "The bastard hit her?" Fury roared through him.

Clayton nodded. "Mary Jane also said that Bree was afraid his abuse might turn to her son. That was the biggest reason she ended the marriage ASAP after the fool roughed her up."

"Wait, wait, wait." Patrick waved his hands back and forth. "Son? Bree has a son?" This was the first he'd heard of that. Damn. She'd had a kid with this bastard. Why hadn't she mentioned having a kid?

Clayton nodded. "I don't know exactly how old he is, but he goes to school."

Bree had married the guy before Patrick moved to Kenner City to go after the position of sheriff. That was six years ago. For all he knew they could have been together awhile before that. Added up, he supposed. If they had the kid early on in the relationship he would be school-age now. Since her husband's name hadn't been Peter, maybe that was the kid's name.

"Anyway, so take it slow, Sheriff," Clayton advised with a look that said you'd better listen up. "She's had a rocky go of it in the relationship arena."

"Thank you, Dr. Phil," Patrick patronized. He pushed to his feet. "Now, if you'll excuse me, I have places to go."

"Wear that blue shirt all the ladies in the office like so much," Clayton called after him.

Right. Like he was going to worry about what the ladies liked.

This was Bree. He didn't have to impress her with fashion.

Tonight would be about getting to know each other again. And moving forward.

It was a good plan.

"TABITHA, you're really cutting it close." Bree rubbed at her forehead. She had a major headache brewing. "I know. I know. Just drive carefully."

Six-thirty.

Bree reminded herself to breathe.

Patrick would be here in thirty minutes and Peter was still here.

"Oh, God."

Bree left the kitchen and went in search of her son. He was curled up on his bed playing a video game.

"You ready to go?"

"Uh-huh," he said as he simultaneously nodded without taking his eyes off the small screen of the handheld game player.

His backpack was on the bed beside

him. He hadn't bothered taking off his shoes. His jacket was close by. He was ready.

But Tabitha wasn't. Layla had run out of gas coming home from a school club meeting.

Roy was out of town with work.

There was no one else to call. Her father couldn't drive anymore. Rarely even left the house.

Of course Layla couldn't be left on the side of the road with an empty gas tank.

Dear Lord.

"Breathe."

Unexpected things came up. Tabitha would get here. She'd already put the gas in Layla's car. She was on her way. It was cool.

Bree walked through the kitchen and living room and looked for signs of her son. Games, books, toys. She'd put everything away.

Like he didn't exist.

She stopped in the middle of the living room and looked around.

"This is ridiculous."

What was she doing?

She would tell Patrick. He deserved to know. More than that, Peter deserved to know. So did Nora.

Just not tonight.

She needed a plan. Going about this the right way was extremely important for all concerned. There were many issues she and Patrick had to resolve before this thing went any further.

Her reasons for keeping Peter a secret in the beginning had been solid. Granted her father had had a heavy hand in the decision. But she had respected him, still did.

Even if he was the one to encourage her to marry Big Jack. Bree stopped. Closed her eyes. Her father wasn't responsible for her decisions. True, she had been vulnerable at the time, but, ultimately, she had made the decision. Jack fooled them all.

This was her mess to straighten out. Not her father's. Not even Jack's. She'd heard rumors of his bad-boy reputation before they'd married. But he'd worked overtime wooing her and she'd fallen for it. He hadn't been the answer to her needs or her son's.

The sound of gravel crunching beneath tires signaled that Tabitha had finally made it.

Thank God.

Bree grabbed her sweater and headed for the door. "Come on, sweetie. Your aunt Tabitha is here. You have to get going."

"Coming!" came the answering shout.

Bree felt weak with relief as she opened the door. "Boy, you about gave me a nervous—" Her brain registered what her eyes saw and her mouth snapped shut.

Tabitha wasn't climbing the steps to Bree's porch. Her minivan was just turning into the drive.

Patrick paused on the top step, glanced back at Tabitha's van then turned a questioning gaze on Bree. He wore a blue shirt that made his eyes look even more startlingly blue. "I'm early, I know, but—"

"Who are you?" Peter ducked under Bree's arm and bounded onto the porch.

Bree's heart nearly stopped.

Patrick stared at the boy. He wouldn't know his name or his age, but he would know his own eyes.

"I'm Peter." He pointed to Bree. "Are you here to see my mom?"

"Come inside, son." Bree was shocked that her voice was steady. She'd gone numb all over. Her legs were barely holding her upright.

Peter looked from Patrick to Bree. "But Aunt Tabitha's here."

Bree managed a stiff nod. "Right. Get your things."

Peter rushed through the doorway via the same route beneath her arm. She'd kept it planted in the door to ensure she remained vertical.

"Is everything all right, Bree?" Tabitha stood at the bottom of the steps. She glanced at Patrick. The worry etched across her face told Bree she was torn between jumping to her sister's defense and taking Peter and running.

"You'll be late for your movie," Bree told her. "Things are fine here."

Peter burst past Bree and jumped off the porch. "Bye, Mom! Bye, mister!"

Tabitha didn't move. She stared at Bree, uncertain what to do.

Bree gestured for her to go. The numbness had abruptly been replaced by staggering emotions she couldn't begin to label. She didn't trust her voice enough to utter a single word.

Tabitha looked back twice before climbing into her van and driving away. Peter waved with both hands. He was completely innocent and oblivious to the tension squeezing the very air from Bree's lungs.

When the van's taillights were out of sight, Bree dared to meet the gaze cutting a hole straight through her heart.

"When did you plan to tell me?"

Patrick's face was hard. Bree had never seen that cold, icy look in his eyes.

"When he graduated from high school?" he demanded.

This was the moment she had dreaded, feared, for nearly eight years. Since the night Peter was born she had mulled over all the things she could or should say to Patrick when the time was right.

None of it would make a difference now.

Nothing she said was going to take that look off his face…or the mixture of disappointment and derision from his eyes.

This wasn't the beginning…it was the end.

Chapter Eight

Patrick settled onto the top step. Standing was no longer possible.

He had a son.

He didn't have to ask the boy's age any more than he had to ask who his father was.

Patrick had stared straight into the same blue eyes he saw in the mirror each morning.

Peter. His son's name was Peter.

Bree had kept this secret for…

Damn. Eight years.

Bree sat down next to him. She braced her arms on her knees. "At the time I thought it was the right thing to do."

Patrick closed his eyes. How could she

have ever, ever thought this was the right thing to do?

"I was young. We…" She inhaled a deep, shaky breath. "You and I had parted on bad terms. My father didn't want me involved with…you."

"Since when did you allow your father to dictate your decisions?" Patrick knew better than that. Bree had always complained about how her mother's entire existence had seemed to revolve around her husband. She hadn't worked outside the home, hadn't even finished school. She'd married young and had children. Ignoring the symptoms so she wouldn't have to be away from her family, she'd waited too late to stop the cancer that ended up taking her life.

"I was pregnant." Bree stared out at the street. "I was afraid."

Afraid? Patrick turned his head, stared at her profile. "You? Afraid? I find that damned hard to believe."

"I don't know what to say."

Bree turned to face him. Her eyes were

bright with emotion. He refused to feel anything but the anger roiling in his gut. She had stolen seven years of his son's life from him. Those years couldn't be gotten back, couldn't be made up. They were gone.

The rumors about Bree's marriage that Clayton had passed along abruptly slammed in Patrick's chest. Fury detonated again. "Did you let that bastard you were married to lay a hand on him?"

Bree shook her head. "Never. I never left him alone with Jack. And I…" She moistened her trembling lips, blinked back the emotion threatening. "He would have had to go through me to get to him."

The rest of what Clayton had told Patrick poked through his anger and sympathy trickled into his veins. "He hurt you?" Patrick didn't have to spell it out. She knew what he meant. If he'd had any doubts the fact that she looked away confirmed it.

"He did." Bree met his gaze once more. "But only once. I left after that."

Patrick tried to hang on to the idea that she'd already suffered enough to help cool his temper, but the realization of what she'd done, not for a month or a year or even two, but for seven long years pushed him over the edge. He lost the battle with his anger. "How could you keep him from me?"

He just couldn't fathom how she'd let so much time pass.

"I kept telling myself it was the right thing to do. You were in Utah. I was here and it…was easier."

"Out of sight, out of mind, right?" That was no excuse. He wasn't going to accept that answer.

"Maybe."

"I've been in Kenner County for six years, Bree. What's your excuse for that?"

The silence lengthened between them. He was beginning to think she wasn't even going to answer when she finally spoke.

"He was one by the time I saw you again. It was…too late. I didn't want to upset his life."

Too late. Patrick shook his head. "Does

he even know who I am?" Of course he didn't. He'd called Patrick mister.

She didn't have to answer that question. He knew.

Patrick stood. He couldn't talk to her anymore. He had to think. To clear his head and reach some place where reason presided.

"We'll finish this…later. I have to think this through."

He walked to his SUV without looking back. If he said anything else, he would likely say something he would regret. He reached for the door, felt ready to explode with frustration.

"Patrick!"

He took a breath, lifted his gaze to her. "What?"

"Dispatch just got a call about a disturbance at the Saloon. The perp is Sherman Watts."

That would mean Watts was drunk. And just maybe he would talk. "Let's go."

Bree dashed into the house and right back out. She strapped her utility belt and weapon around her hips as she rushed to his SUV.

Patrick started the engine and rammed into reverse. "Just so you know," he said, "I won't let you keep my son from me any longer."

THE KENNER CITY SALOON was a bar designed like an old Western saloon. Not Sherman Watts's typical hangout. Bree knew from the times in the past that she or one of her colleagues had picked him up he generally liked the sleazier joints.

Patrick pulled to the curb at the front entrance. A number of patrons were already milling around on the sidewalk.

"'Bout time the po' got here," someone said loud enough for Bree to hear.

Patrick hesitated at the double entry doors. "No heroics," he warned.

Bree didn't respond, just went inside. Her mind was whirling with this evening's events. She couldn't deal with anything else right now.

At least nothing personal.

Inside most of the remaining patrons were huddled in a corner discussing what was going down.

The saloon's one bouncer, dressed in a black tee that designated him as security, had Watts cornered at one end of the long bar.

"I don't care how many cops you call," Watts shouted at the bouncer. "I'm not going nowhere until I get my drink."

"Mr. Watts, the bartender cut you off. You can either take a taxi home or you can go with the cops when they get here."

Patrick entered Watts's line of sight and propped on the bar. "Maybe the man will settle down if he gets his drink."

The bouncer looked at Patrick as if he'd lost his mind. "You for real, Sheriff?"

Patrick eased onto the closest stool. "Absolutely. I'll make sure Mr. Watts gets home."

The bouncer shrugged and walked away.

Watts swaggered over to the bar and pounded the top. "Give me that JD!"

Bree didn't sit. She crossed her arms over her chest and glared at Watts. "Sounds like your taste in whiskey has changed for the better, Sherman. Since when did you bother with anything that has a reputable label?"

The bartender slapped a glass on the counter. Watts picked it up, lifted it high as if toasting Bree. "That's right. I'm all about moving up."

Bree despised this lowlife. He should be tossed into the pokey and the key be thrown away. "Why don't you do us all a favor and move right on up to Montana or someplace like that?"

Watts laughed. "Maybe I will. This place is going to the dogs." He sneered at her. "Nothing but bitches to pick from."

"Watch yourself, Watts," Patrick cautioned.

Bree had let this guy's name-calling go when they interviewed him at his friend's trailer. Considering what she'd already been through this evening, she wasn't taking any grief from him tonight.

"I guess you thought Julie Grainger was

a bitch, too," Bree suggested. She hated that word. Hated scumbags like Watts who just kept repeating the same crimes over and over until they got bored and escalated to something worse. Like rape or murder.

Watts's expression sobered instantly. "I don't know what you're talking about, Detective. I told you I didn't know that fed."

"We have a witness who says you did," Patrick countered. "That you were engaged in a heated exchange with Grainger only a few days before she was murdered. That makes you a person of interest to this case."

Watts shook his head drunkenly. "The only heated exchange I'd like to do is with your sidekick here." He hitched a thumb in Bree's direction. "You nailed that yet, Sheriff?"

The next thing that happened startled Bree so that she could only stand there, stunned.

Patrick jumped off the stool, grabbed Watts by the lapels of his shirt and jerked him close. "How about I nail your ass to the wall for murder? You could make all kinds of friends in prison."

Two Kenner City officers charged into the saloon at that moment. Lucky for Patrick. Bree was pretty sure he was about to cross a line he knew better than to cross. Her emotions were raw, his no doubt were as well. He wasn't thinking rationally.

"Take this piece of crap in for drunk and disorderly conduct," Patrick instructed one of the officers as he shoved Watts toward the other one. He glanced at the bartender. "I guess he won't need that drink after all."

The bartender shrugged and took the glass away.

Watts laughed as the officer cuffed him. "You shouldda slugged me while you had the chance, Sheriff. Maybe you don't have the guts to be a man."

"Come on, Watts." The officer pushed Watts into motion.

The second officer started reading Watts his rights.

"I know my rights," the jerk muttered.

As he was hauled past Bree, Watts

stalled. "You come on down to the jail and see me, little girl. I like squaws."

Watts laughed like the idiot he was as the officers hauled him from the saloon. The huddled patrons watched until he was gone then took their places once more. The night was young, they still had drinking and partying and celebrating to do.

Bree walked out of the saloon. She was spent emotionally. She needed to go home and forget this day had happened. She'd had more than enough grief and worry and anger for one day.

She dragged out her cell and called her sister. Gave her location and closed the phone. The last thing she wanted to do was climb back into that vehicle with Patrick. She couldn't take anymore tonight. She couldn't bear the way he looked at her.

"I can take you home." He paused next to her.

She turned to him, looked him square in the eyes. "No. You can't. We both need to think. I can't deal with anything else."

"I'm not leaving you standing out here like this."

Bree threw her hands up. "It's a public street, Patrick. There are lots of lights and people all over the place. My sister will be here in fifteen minutes. Just go home and leave me alone."

She was perfectly capable of taking care of herself. Fury twisted inside her. She just wanted this night to be over. She wanted to hold her son in her arms until she fell asleep and then to forget this day ever happened.

Patrick got into his SUV but didn't drive away until her sister's minivan arrived.

Bree settled into the passenger seat.

"You okay?"

Bree couldn't answer. If she spoke, if she even looked at Tabitha, she would burst into tears.

Because she was not okay.

PATRICK PARKED in front of the Morning Ray Café. He couldn't go home. He'd thought he could, but he couldn't.

He had to talk to someone.

The only person who could possibly understand was his mother.

Nora Martinez lived above the little restaurant that had been her saving grace. She'd been telling Patrick that since he was a kid. After his father had died she'd needed something. Her only child was in school everyday and didn't need so much of her time and attention. Nora had needed this to fill in the gaps.

Patrick had come home from school to his mother's warm hugs and the smell of home-cooked meals and desserts. She'd worked hard to be mother and father. Still did.

She would understand and be able to explain what he was feeling.

The ache in his soul was something he had never experienced before. He kept seeing that little boy with those big blue eyes.

His boy.

The one who didn't even know his name.

He climbed from his SUV and shuffled

to the door. Exhaustion clawed at him. Not a physical weariness, but an emotional one.

He pressed the buzzer that let his mother know when after-hours deliveries arrived. He had a key but he didn't want to startle her.

It took a minute or two but soon she was padding across the tiled floor in her robe and house slippers. She worked hard all day being the perfect hostess and chef. The nights were her haven from the noise and the crowd. Though she loved every minute of it, she needed her down time as well.

She shoved the key into the plate glass door, her face puckered in confusion.

"Is something wrong, son?"

Only everything.

But he wasn't a little boy anymore, he was a grown man. Crying was out of the question, though he felt exactly like doing exactly that.

"I need to talk."

"Well, come on in." She took him by the arm and tugged him inside. "You want some coffee?" She locked the door and turned to him. "Something to eat?"

He wasn't sure he could deal with food or even anything to drink. He just needed her to listen and help him make sense of this…this news.

He shook his head.

"Well, come on, let's go upstairs. I'll turn my DVR off. I can watch my soaps another time."

That made him smile. His mother was addicted to the daytime soaps. She had been for as long as he could remember.

Upstairs she settled on the comfy old sofa she'd had forever. "Sit down, Patrick." Her brow furrowed with worry. "It can't be that bad."

He lowered into the chair directly across from her. "It's…not good." That felt like the wrong thing to say. Learning that he had a son wasn't wrong…it was everything else that was not right.

"It's about Bree, isn't it?"

His mother had always been able to read him like a book. "Yeah, it's about Bree."

Nora curled her legs under her and sank deeper into the big cushions. "Start at the beginning, Patrick. You know how I hate it when you leave out parts."

Where exactly was the beginning? Their relationship had ended eight years ago. But Nora knew all about that. No need to start that far back.

"When Bree and I ended our relationship, she was pregnant."

Surprise flared in his mother's eyes. "Oh."

"Yeah. Oh." He scrubbed his hands over his face and wished he knew how to feel about this. Mad. Sick. Disgusted. Anything would be better than this turmoil of emotions playing tug of war inside him.

"Obviously, she didn't tell you," Nora guessed.

He moved his head from side to side. "I found out tonight when I saw my seven-year-old son for the first time."

Her breath caught.

"He…he looks just like I did when I was

a kid." Patrick stared at his hands. "Same hair. Same eyes. Everything."

"Did Bree say why she didn't tell you?"

It didn't matter why. It was wrong, no matter the excuse. "She said she thought, at the time, it was the right thing to do. Her father didn't want me in the picture. Probably because I'm not Ute. She did what he told her."

Nora digested that information for a moment. "And you don't believe that?"

He dropped his head back on the chair. "For as long as I've known Bree she was her own woman. She doesn't take any grief from anyone and she definitely doesn't let anyone tell her how to live her life."

"But," Nora cut in before he could continue, "she was young. Pregnant. And scared."

Bree had said that.

Patrick just couldn't swallow that excuse. "She's the most fearless female I know." He met his mother's gaze. "Besides you. That's a cop-out if I've ever heard one. She just didn't want to tell me. To punish me or something."

Nora shrugged. "Maybe a little, but you don't know how it feels to wake up one day and learn you're carrying another life inside you, Patrick. It's an overwhelming rush of anticipation and excitement and most of all fear. Every decision you make, every move you make, even what you eat and drink affects that tiny life growing inside you. It's a humbling experience, dear. I'm certain she was terrified. Especially considering the two of you had ended your relationship on such bad terms."

How could his mother take her side? "Okay, so maybe she was scared at first. But what about a year later. Or two years later? We're talking more than seven here, Mom, and I still wouldn't have known if I hadn't shown up at her house early tonight."

Nora's face softened. "What's his name?"

Patrick closed his eyes and envisioned his son. "Peter."

Nora repeated the name. "I like that."

She settled her gaze onto Patrick's. "There's only one thing to do."

He was all ears.

"You and Bree have to work this out. The important thing here is the boy. He needs both of you and you both deserve to be a part of his life. So, do whatever it takes but work it out."

That was a lot of help. "How am I supposed to do that?"

"Well, that's simple. Patrick, my mother had an old saying about moments like this."

There she went with her mother's sage advice. "Mom—"

"If you're walking down the road and you come upon a mule in the ditch—" she turned her palms up "—you don't ask why the mule is in the ditch, you just get it out."

"What does a mule have to do with the fact that I'm a father and nobody bothered to tell me?" He needed clarification not more confusion.

"You have to get that mule out of the ditch, Patrick. Remember, it doesn't matter why it's in the ditch, you just have to get it out. Wasting time wondering why is just that, a waste. We have a tendency to waste a lot of time wondering why. Why are we too short or too fat? Why are prices so high? Why don't we make enough money? Why does so-and-so have this or that? Don't waste any more time. Get the mule out of the ditch, son."

As if his thoughts and feelings had suddenly all lined up and fell right into place, he knew exactly what he had to do. He smiled weakly at his mother. "You're the smartest woman I know."

"I'm not smart, son. I've just lived a lot more years than you." Nora pressed a hand to her chest. "I have a grandson."

And Patrick was a father.

A father who wanted to be a part of his son's life. All he had to do was get that mule out of the ditch.

He thought about the way he'd reacted tonight. And of how afraid and vulnerable Bree must have been to make the decision she made.

The why didn't matter…all that mattered was his son.

And Bree.

They would work this out.

Tomorrow morning he would call her and make the first move. He would give her tonight to think about things. Then they would form a plan.

Pride wasn't going to get in the way of doing the right thing.

Patrick was man enough to admit that what happened eight years ago was as much his fault as Bree's. He wouldn't give her another reason to run from him or to avoid him.

Even if they were never anything more than friends, their son had to come first.

He'd been right about needing to mend fences. Tomorrow he would take the first step.

Chapter Nine

Bree stood at the kitchen sink, the coffee she held getting cold.

She stared at nothing in particular. Her son's swing set in the backyard…the picnic table they used so much during the summer months.

In a few minutes it would be time to wake her son to get ready for school. For now she continued to stand there feeling empty and so tired.

Sleep had been impossible. Her sister had brought Peter home around ten-thirty. She'd wanted to talk and to comfort Bree, but Bree hadn't been able to talk. Her emotions had been too raw.

Tabitha had finally, reluctantly gone

home. But she'd left Bree with one piece of advice. *"Remember, after every storm comes the calm."*

Bree wasn't so sure about that this time.

This was like a massive earthquake that had hit, ripping open her life and tossing every aspect this way and that. An earthquake she had known for years was coming and still she hadn't been prepared.

Patrick was hurt and angry. She could understand that. He had no intention of being left out of his son's life again. And she understood that, as well. But because of the way he'd found out—no, that wasn't right. Because of what she had done, deceiving him for all these years, their relationship would be strained. He would never trust her again. How could she blame him?

There was absolutely no way to make this right.

Fear and uncertainty had prompted her to make the wrong decision. Selfishness and the feeling of being in too deep to turn back had kept her making those same decisions.

Now everyone would pay the price.

Her cell vibrated and she pulled it from its holster. Dispatch.

"Hunter."

"Detective Hunter, the sheriff's department called. Sheriff Martinez needs you to meet him ASAP."

God, had there been another murder? Bree's first thought was that something had happened to Agent Ben Parrish. He seemed to be high on everyone's suspect list at the moment. If Parrish was somehow involved with the bad guys in this case, she imagined his colleagues at the Bureau were the least of his worries.

"Give me the location." Bree grabbed the pen and pad on the counter and jotted down the directions. "Thanks. I'm on my way."

Bree stared at the location. Pretty much a deserted canyon area. Images from the desolate place where Grainger's body had been found filtered through her mind. *Don't let it be another murder.*

She tucked her phone away and glanced at the clock—6:15 a.m. She would need to get Peter up a few minutes early. Tabitha or Layla would have to take him to school. Bree didn't know what she would do without her family's support. She couldn't fathom how single moms with no network of family or friends survived.

Patrick wouldn't have asked her to meet him like this unless it was important. She supposed he had dispatch call her because he hadn't wanted to speak directly to her. Not that she could blame him. She'd had her reasons for making the decisions she had made. He had his reasons for reacting the way he was now. They were only human and they would both have to come to terms with those feelings.

Bree called her sister who promised to be there in fifteen minutes. Thankfully Tabitha had always been an early riser.

Setting her coffee aside, Bree summoned her missing-in-action courage and pushed away all the uncertainty and niggling fears. It was time to stop whining and fretting about it and face the music. She had a job to do and a life to live.

That was the thing. Agent Grainger had lost her life way too early. She'd been so young. Bree wasn't about to take another moment of hers for granted. This thing with Patrick would work out in time.

Meanwhile she should get her son up and moving. She never liked to leave without giving him a hug and telling him she loved him.

For a moment she stood at the door to his bedroom and watched him sleep. So trusting, so peaceful. His little world was about to change. But it would be for the better. He wanted a father in his life. Now he would have a good one.

One who might never forgive Bree, but Patrick would be an outstanding father.

Further proof she had made the wrong decisions.

Enough. No looking back, only forward.

"Peter." She shook him gently. "Time to get ready for school."

His eyes opened and he frowned. "Not yet."

"Yes, yet," Bree scolded. "Your aunt

Tabitha will be here soon and you need to be up and dressed.

Peter frowned. "Do you have to go to work early?"

Bree nodded. "I have to meet the sheriff and I can't be late."

"Okay." Peter got up and dragged himself across the hall to the bathroom.

Bree went back to the kitchen to make his favorite breakfast. Toast and cereal. He preferred picking out his own clothes for the day. Like his father, Peter had very strong ideas about his likes and dislikes.

Five minutes later Tabitha arrived.

Bree was all set to say good morning and get going but Tabitha waylaid her. "There's something I need to tell you."

Bree glanced at the clock. "Make it fast. I really have to go."

"Yesterday after Layla picked Peter up from school they came by here for a couple of hours so he could work on his science project."

The project was due next week. Her son

was required to do it all on his own, no help from parents. Bree had no idea what exactly he was doing on his computer but he assured her it was almost finished.

"Did something happen?" Bree didn't like the new kind of worry she saw in her sister's eyes. Bree's problems seemed to be piling up on her sister and that wasn't fair. How would she ever repay Tabitha for all that she'd done?

"Sort of. Layla said it had happened a couple of times before." Tabitha shrugged. "Last week, I think. But last night was different. The phone rang three different times in the space of two hours."

"What do you mean the phone rang? Who called?"

"That's just it, whoever it was kept hanging up when Layla said hello. It was weird. She didn't mention it to me until last night."

"I'll look into it." Bree's instincts warned that it was the same person who was watching her. Who'd left her that warning. She couldn't play off this situation any longer. She had to start taking it a lot more seriously.

"One more thing, Bree."

"Tabitha, honey, I really gotta go."

"I know. I know." Tabitha put her hand on Bree's arm. "Just remember that Patrick is a good man. A really good man. He'll get over his anger and come to terms with the decisions you made."

Bree could only hope.

"Besides—" Tabitha smiled "—Peter is going to be thrilled to have a daddy who's a sheriff. That's pretty cool for a boy, you know."

"That's true." Bree hugged her sister. "Okay, I gotta go. Otherwise the sheriff is going to be mad at me for being late. We don't need to add fuel to the fire."

"Go," Tabitha urged.

Bree called bye to her son and had made it to the porch, hit the button on the remote to unlock the SUV's doors and realized she had better make a bathroom run before heading out. There were no bathrooms in the canyons.

Back in the house, Bree did her business, washed her hands and checked her reflection. She felt calmer now. She could do this. Patrick wasn't a bear. He was a good guy. A man she had once loved…still loved on some level.

This would all work out…eventually.

Bree repeated her goodbyes as she passed through the living room and out the door.

Patrick would be waiting…and maybe another body.

PATRICK PACED the distance between his SUV and the road entering the canyon one more time.

Why had Bree wanted him to meet her here?

If a crime had been committed there was no indication. No official vehicles. No Bree. No victim.

If she wanted to talk to him she'd picked a hell of a place. They certainly wouldn't be interrupted.

He set his hands on his hips and did a

three-sixty survey of the canyon. They would definitely have privacy.

There had to be a mistake. He fished his cell phone from his jacket pocket. It was damned chilly to be meeting outside like this for anything other than official business.

He'd just entered Bree's cell number and gotten the no service message when a cloud of dust appeared in the distance.

Now he would find out what was going on. Patrick put his phone away and waited for Bree to reach his position and park.

She climbed out of the SUV, her gaze colliding with his. "What's going on?"

A frown worried his brow. "I was about to ask you the same thing."

Bree stopped a few steps away, turned all the way around to survey their surroundings. "What do you mean?" She searched his face. "You asked me to meet you here."

Wait. "No. You asked me to meet you here."

What the hell was going on?

Patrick took another long look around.

The craggy cliffs that surrounded the canyon had snow hanging on the tops. Sprigs of desert grass managed to survive here and there. A couple of old mine shafts were boarded up. One had been vandalized with spray paint and a couple of the boards serving as a barrier to the opening were missing. "I think we've been set up."

"By who?"

Patrick rubbed his hand over his jaw, his instincts moving to the next level. "I don't think we're deep enough into the Grainger case for it to be about that." Sherman Watts crossed his mind. This could be his way of getting even.

No, that couldn't be right. That weasel would likely still be in jail this morning. Unless one of his buddies had gotten him released. Funny thing was, Watts didn't really have any friends. Not real friends. He had drinking and gambling buddies. Certainly none had the means to post bail.

"I'm calling dispatch to find out what's going on here," Bree said, reaching for her cell phone.

"No service," Patrick warned.

The rear door of Bree's borrowed SUV opened. Patrick's hand was on the butt of his weapon in a heartbeat.

Bree whirled around, her own hand going to her weapon as well.

"Where are we?" Bree's son, Peter, bailed out of the backseat. "I never been here before."

"Peter!" Bree rushed to her son and crouched down to his level. "What were you doing hiding in there? Your aunt Tabitha will be worried sick. You have to go to school."

Bree stood, reached for her cell. Huffed a breath of frustration when she saw that Patrick was right, no service. Bree shook her head. "Tabitha will be scared to death."

Patrick's gaze settled on the boy. His heart started to pound. The child looked like a carbon copy of him at that age.

"Peter." Bree shook her head. "You shouldn't have sneaked off from your aunt Tabitha." She stared at the cell phone in her hand as if she'd forgotten what she was supposed to do next. "I…I need to call dispatch and find out what's going on." But she couldn't…no damned service.

Patrick looked from her to the boy. He couldn't stop staring at him. He was—

"Are you my daddy?"

The impact of the question slammed Patrick square in the chest. He looked from the boy to Bree. What was he supposed to say?

Bree looked as terrified and confused as Patrick.

A snap, then a far too familiar ring echoed through the canyon.

Rifle shot.

"Get down!"

Bree was already flying to the ground, her body shielding her son as she took him down with her.

Patrick hit the dirt.

The next shot sent a puff of dust into the air not two feet from his head.

He'd hoped the first shot was a mistake.

But that wasn't the case.

Someone was shooting at them.

Chapter Ten

Bree tried to roll, with Peter in tow, toward her vehicle. A bullet pinged into the side of her SUV.

Peter wailed. "Mommy!"

Damn. Bree's heart threatened to burst from her chest. She had to do something.

"Head for the rocks," Patrick shouted. "I'll cover you."

"Come on, baby," Bree urged, her throat so dry she could hardly speak. "Crawl with Mommy."

Ensuring Peter stayed beneath her, Bree moved onto all fours and started the slow, treacherous journey toward the base of the mountain. Patrick returned fire. The thundering sounds echoing over and over before fading into the distance.

God, she had to hurry. When he had to reload…

Bree made it to the first pile of boulders. Thank God.

She pulled Peter into her arms and huddled behind the rock mass.

One second, then two of silence sent a new rush of adrenaline searing through her veins.

Patrick. He'd had to stop firing to reload.

The distinct rifle bursts pierced the air.

She couldn't just sit here. She had to do something.

First, call for backup. Instinctively, she reached for her phone. Wouldn't help. "Damn!"

Okay, okay, think. She had to make sure Peter was safe and then she had to give Patrick backup. Shots from his .40 caliber service weapon popped loudly in punctuation of her reasoning.

Bree surveyed the area behind their hiding place. The base of the mountain.

Cracks and crevices. Wait. An old mine shaft. It was boarded up but some of the boards were missing. She visually measured the distance. They could make it.

"Peter, listen to me."

Her son was sobbing. His body shook with fear.

"It's okay, sweetie. We're gonna keep you safe. Now listen to me, okay? It's really important."

Watery blue eyes peered up at her.

"You see that hole over there between the boards?" She pointed to the spot.

Peter nodded. "A cave?"

"Sort of." Gold and silver mining had been rampant in these mountains and canyons during the nineteenth century. Peter had learned about those in school but he was scared right now and not thinking clearly.

"I'm going to hide you in there so I can help the sheriff, okay?"

Peter didn't look to sure of that. "You can't stay with me?"

"I have to help, son."

He nodded. "Okay."

Bree peeked beyond the enormous boulder that protected them from the shooter's view. Patrick had rolled close to his SUV. He couldn't possibly have any more clips handy. There was always one in the weapon and another on the utility belt.

She had to do something. Fast.

"Come on, baby." Bree pulled her son close. "Let's get you to a safe place."

Bree decided on a route that took the most advantage of every boulder and rock between their position and the opening she needed to reach.

"When I start moving," Bree instructed her son, "you stay under Mommy like before." He was getting to be a big boy. But she could shield his body fairly well even if it did make moving difficult. "Remember not to stop unless I stop."

She got a shaky nod in reply.

Bree got into position. "Let's go."

Moving together, they half crawled, half scooted across the cool dirt and rocks. The rifle shots were interspersed between Patrick's louder blasts. If the shooter was still aiming for Patrick that meant he hadn't noticed their movements.

Please, God, let Patrick keep him occupied.

A thud hit the dirt right on her heels. She didn't have to look back to know she and Peter were now targets.

"Faster, baby," she urged as her arms and legs frantically worked to propel them forward.

The last dive for the opening between the boards was accompanied by two pings into the rock right next to the opening.

Damned close.

She urged Peter deep into the darkness.

"It's dark, Mommy."

"Keep going. It'll be all right."

When she felt they were a safe distance inside, she reached for the flashlight on her belt. "You can hold this but don't turn it on unless you absolutely have to. And turn it that way." She wrapped his shaking hands around the flashlight and pointed it away from the opening they'd entered.

She collapsed on her butt. Her arms and legs were trembling.

They were okay.

For now.

Patrick.

She had to make sure he was okay.

"Stay right here, sweetie," she implored. "I'm gonna check on the sheriff."

"No." Peter grabbed her jacket. "Don't go back out there."

Bree hugged her son, fought the tears. "I have to help, baby. You know that. It's my job."

When Peter had calmed a bit, she gave him another tight hug. "Stay right here. Be very quiet. And I'll be back before you know it."

"Okay." His voice was thin and high-pitched. He was scared to death.

Bree made her way back to the opening. Though she couldn't see much of anything she was pretty sure this was a shaft that had been used in the early, primitive mining days. Which could mean it wasn't the safest place to hide. But right now she had no choice.

She paused in the shadows near the opening. Listened. Patrick's .40 caliber popped off another round. He was close. He must have sought cover nearer to her location.

Another rifle ping landed near the rocks where she and Peter had first taken refuge. The shooter was coming closer. He likely knew Patrick would soon be out of ammo.

"Patrick!" Normally she wouldn't call out and give her location away, but the shooter already knew exactly where she was.

"Stay where you are!" Patrick commanded.

Could she throw a clip hard enough to reach his position? Bree chewed her lower lip, tried to gauge the distance.

Maybe.

"I'm going to toss you my extra clip," she called out to him.

A ping zapped the edge of the opening. She jerked her head back.

"Stay back!" Patrick shouted, his voice gruff.

Bree ignored his warning. She grabbed the clip from her belt, waited for the next rifle shot.

She thrust her upper body through the opening and threw the clip as hard as she could.

Drawing quickly back inside, she shouted, "I tossed it near the three rocks clustered together."

"Stay out of sight, Bree!"

She'd done all she could.

Now she waited.

Until Patrick nailed the son of a bitch. Or backup arrived. Though they didn't have cell service, Tabitha would be frantic to get in touch with Bree. She would call dispatch and dispatch would send someone to this location.

If neither of those things happened she would be forced to stay put...until the bastard came charging into this shaft.

Bree crawled back to where Peter huddled. She positioned herself in front of him, braced her arms on her bent knees and took aim at the opening.

If the shooter came through that opening he was a dead man.

PATRICK SCRAMBLED toward the cluster of rocks. Hit the ground on his belly and snatched up the clip.

Two, three bullets rained around him like hail.

He rolled back to take cover behind the larger boulder.

There was no choice at this point but to wait the bastard out. If he thought he'd hit Patrick he might just come closer enough to kill.

Fury tightened Patrick's lips.

He'd only just learned of his son's existence. And Bree. Bree was back in his life, on shaky ground but back nonetheless. No son of a bitch was going to take that from him.

He opened his cell phone again and tried to get a call through.

Not enough service.

Dammit.

The next rifle shot sounded a hell of a lot closer.

Patrick smiled.

"Come on, you bastard," he muttered.

Patrick braced his back against the boulder, knees bent, hands wrapped around his weapon.

A muscle started to flex in his jaw in the ensuing silence.

"Come on."

A rumble echoed in the canyon.

What the hell?

Patrick tensed. Listened hard.

Definitely not a weapon firing. Not vehicles arriving, though that would be nice as hell.

Another thundering rumble.

And then he knew.

The cave or old mine shaft.

His chest seized.

Another fierce rumble reverberated around him.

Dust flew from the opening of the abandoned mine shaft where Bree and Peter had sought refuge.

Terror lit in Patrick's veins.

He shot to his feet, not caring about the danger, and charged toward the opening.

Another dust cloud burst free of the rocks.

Then there was silence.

Patrick stilled.

His heart swelled in his chest until he thought it would explode.

He started forward again.

"Don't move."

Patrick froze.

"One more step and you're dead."

Chapter Eleven

Bree coughed hard. She scrambled up.

Peter?

She shook her baby gently. She'd been lying flat on top of him.

"Baby?"

He whimpered.

Thank God.

"Are you okay, baby?"

"It hurts." He moaned.

Oh, God.

The flashlight. She needed the flashlight!

She felt around where he lay. Where was it?

He moaned softly and started to sob.

"Just let me find the flashlight, sweetie, and Mommy will take care of you." Her heart pounded like a drum inside her rib cage.

"I got it," he mumbled. Peter bumped her with the flashlight.

Relief flooded her. "You did good, baby." Thank God. Thank God.

She clicked on the flashlight and started her examination. Tears spilled from his eyes and his face was contorted with pain but there was no blood. No sign of injury around his head and neck.

"Where do you hurt, baby?" Torso area was also clear of blood. No visible injuries.

"My leg." He cried out. "Oh, my leg!"

The ache that bloomed inside her forced her to swallow a moan.

She guided the light to his legs. "I'm going to touch your legs one at a time, okay?" He moaned but didn't protest further.

She moved her fingers gently down his right leg. No protests. Nothing felt out of the ordinary. Now for the left one.

The instant her fingers touched his left thigh he cried out. "It's okay. I'll be very careful."

Her pulse hammered. All the possibilities, including internal blood loss, if something major was broken badly enough, raced through her mind.

"You tell me if the part I'm touching hurts." She moved slowly down the thigh. Then over the knee. When her fingers eased down his calf, he screamed.

Bree jerked her hand back. "It's okay, it's okay." Tears streamed down her dusty cheeks. She leaned carefully over him and pressed her cheek to his. "It's not so bad," she promised. She tried hard not to allow her voice to shake but she wasn't entirely successful.

She checked him over once more. Hips and pelvis were clear of blood.

She raised up once more. "Okay, baby, I'm going to touch you, starting with your head. You tell me if anything else hurts, okay?"

Please, God, don't let there be any more collapsing in this shaft.

Peter whimpered through the examination but insisted that nothing hurt but his leg. His reflexes appeared fine. Pupils were a little dilated but that could be from the fear. Or the consuming darkness beyond the flashlight's beam.

Hell, she didn't know.

Everything she'd learned in her emergency training course was suddenly out the window.

If she had a knife. Scissors. Anything she could use to remove the pants leg and check out the damage. But she didn't dare move him.

She sat back on her haunches. Tried to think. "I'm going to check your feet. Is that all right? I'll be really careful."

"Don't make it hurt more, Mommy, please."

Why couldn't it have been her? She'd give anything to take away his pain.

"I'll do my best."

She swallowed. Her throat was so dry it hurt. With painstaking care she untied and wiggled off his right shoe. "Everything okay here?" she asked as she palpitated his foot.

"Yes." He moaned.

"Let's try the other one."

Bree untied the left shoe, then held her breath as she slowly removed it. She examined his foot. "Doesn't hurt here?"

He moved his head from side to side.

"Good." She wished she could examine his calf more closely. The best she could tell there might be a compound fracture. There was a significant lump about midway down the length of his calf. Felt like the bone was split completely apart but there was no dampness to indicate it had pierced the skin.

But what did she know? She was a cop!

Stay calm. If Peter sensed she was upset, it would make him more upset. She had to be brave so he could be brave.

"Are we gonna get outta here?" he asked softly.

Fear made her tremble. "Of course we are. Patrick is right outside. I'll bet he's already getting help." If he was still alive.

Bree closed her eyes and forced the images away. Agent Grainger's face kept swimming in front of her eyes.

No. Patrick couldn't be dead.

They were all going to be fine.

Think like a cop, Bree. Don't think like a victim or a mother. Think like a cop.

"I'm going to get as close to the opening as I can and call out to Patrick. Maybe he'll hear me."

Peter's sobs grew frantic. "Don't leave me."

"I'll be right over there. You'll be able to see the flashlight." They weren't more than twelve or fifteen feet from where the opening had been.

"No!" he wailed.

"It's like when you were younger and I'd check your closet," she assured him. "You would be on the bed and you could see me across the room looking in the closet. Okay?"

He nodded jerkily.

Bree took her time, scrambled over the debris. Her senses were ever alert for the slightest sound or filtering of dust that might indicate another collapse was imminent. Thank God she'd recognized what the rumbling meant in time to cover Peter's body. Evidently a falling rock had hit his leg where it lay between hers. She'd pretty much sprawled over him in an effort to protect his trunk and head.

When she'd gone as far as she could, she turned the flashlight beam to the side and looked for any sign of light that might be creeping through.

Nothing.

Did that mean they would run out of oxygen?

Wasn't that the worry when a mine collapsed?

Stop. They weren't underground. This wasn't the same kind of situation. They were going to be fine. Patrick would get them out of here.

Bree took a deep breath, coughed hard. When her lungs had stopped seizing, she took another deep breath and called out, "Patrick!"

She listened for any sound. Nothing. All she could hear was blood roaring in her ears.

"Patrick!"

Still nothing.

There was no way she could dig her way out of here. The rocks were too large. Moving one might start more trouble.

Bree took a moment to calm herself. She couldn't let Peter see her mounting fear.

When she'd pulled herself together again, she crawled over the rocks and debris to where he lay.

"Doing okay?"

He nodded. His eyes were puffy from crying. Bree glanced back at the mass of rocks that lay between them and freedom. For now there was nothing she could do but hope help would reach them soon.

Except… She peered down at her son. She could try to make him feel better.

Bree crept around to his right to lie next to him. It was a lumpy bed but she didn't care. She laid the flashlight between them, letting the beam light up their faces.

"Just think," she said, "when your friends hear about this they're going to be thinking you're a superhero."

Peter made a sound that might have been a laugh.

She swiped the hair from his face, wiped his damp cheeks. "I'll bet none of your friends have ever done this."

He shook his head. "I'll be the only one."

Bree smiled. "You sure will."

Peter licked his lips. "Is that man really my daddy?"

Bree's lashes brimmed with tears once more. "Yes. He's your daddy. His name is Patrick Martinez. He's the sheriff of Kenner County." Dear God, she had made such a tragic mistake.

"He's a good guy then, not like Big Jack."

"Not at all like Jack," Bree agreed.

"He looks like me."

Bree laughed. "Yes, he does." So very, very much.

"Has he caught a lot of bad guys like you?"

"Even more." Pride replaced some of the pain in her chest. "All the good people in Four Corners, especially in Kenner County, love your daddy."

Peter turned his face to hers. "Do you love him like Robby's mom loves his dad?"

The tears won the battle and rolled past her lashes. "Yes, I do."

"Tell me stories about my daddy," Peter said. "It makes me feel better to hear you talk."

"Sure, baby." She wiggled a little closer. "I'll tell you all the stories you want to hear. And the next thing you know help will be here."

Please, God, don't let her be wrong.

"DROP YOUR GUN."

Patrick considered his options. He could toss his weapon and get shot in the back. Or he could make a dive for cover and get shot anyway.

He'd go for Plan C. Even though he didn't exactly have a Plan C.

"If we don't get help," he said slowly, "Bree and her son will die in there. They may be hurt."

The bastard behind him laughed. "Maybe you don't get it yet, but that's the point. I've been planning ways to kill that bitch for months now. I took my time, though. Wanted to give her a good scare first."

"You must be the ex." At least the question of who was harassing Bree was solved.

"That's right. And if I can't have her no one else will. Just knowing she's breathing makes me sick."

Patrick had to make a move. He had to do something. Bree and Peter could be hurt. It would take time for help to get here and time was wasting.

Patrick wasn't about to lose either one of them. "Why don't we talk about this rationally? So far you're only guilty of harassment. You let them die in there and it'll be murder. I don't think you really want to spend the rest of your life in prison."

"Who says I'm going to prison?"

He had moved closer. Patrick braced himself for action.

"Well, since you left your prints all over

her SUV," Patrick lied, "it'll be a simple matter to tie you to this."

"But I didn't leave any prints."

He was coming closer.

"Are you sure? The crime lab says differently."

Hesitation.

He was trying to remember if he'd made a mistake. "No way," he finally said. "No way. And I made all those calls from public phones. I wore gloves when I left that message on her SUV. I got friends who'll swear I was with them this morning. No way I can be tied to any of it."

Patrick laughed. Thankfully it didn't sound as nervous as he felt. "I wouldn't count on any of your friends. We've been talking to a few of them and they were only too willing to share what you've been up to." Patrick was taking a risk bluffing like this. But, at this point, he had nothing to lose.

"I said drop your weapon." The business end of the rifle rammed into his back.

Patrick flinched. He had to wrap this

up. If Bree or Peter were hurt… "All right. No need to get excited."

"I am excited," he growled, leaning close to the back of Patrick's head. "I want to watch from up on those cliffs as they cart her body out of that damned hole. It would've been more fun to shoot her between the eyes, but this'll work."

Patrick stiffened. The images the bastard's words evoked made his gut clench.

"Now drop it."

Patrick bent at the knees and slowly lowered into a crouch to do as the man said. "I'm putting my weapon down. Just stay cool."

Patrick placed the weapon on the ground.

Uncurled his fingers from around it.

This was it.

Act or die.

Since Patrick had no intention of dying today, he opted to act.

He propelled his body into a spin, crashed into the bastard's legs and twisted.

The impact threw the man off balance.

The bastard flew backwards. The rifle discharged into the air.

Patrick got a swing in, an uppercut to his jaw. He grunted but recovered quickly. He rammed a fist into Patrick's chest. Patrick groaned, went for his throat.

They rolled. One minute Patrick was on top, the next the bastard was.

But Patrick had something going for him that this bastard didn't have. Sheer desperation.

Patrick got astride him and punched him in the face. He grunted. Patrick thought of how this bastard had hurt Bree and threatened Peter and he punched him over and over until he was no longer moving.

Patrick couldn't stop. He kept seeing this guy hurt Bree.

Harder and harder he rammed his fist into the bastard's face.

Stop. Patrick hesitated, his fist halfway to the bastard's nose again.

Enough. Getting to Bree and Peter was more important than beating this guy to death.

Patrick retrieved a pair of nylon cuffs from his SUV and secured his prisoner.

For good measure he kicked him in the side. A grunting sound escaped his mouth though he was clearly unconscious.

Patrick left the guy lying there and went in search of his cell phone. He opened it, glowered at the lack of signal bars.

"Dammit!" He'd forgotten. No damned service.

He rushed to the opening that had collapsed and called Bree's name. No answer. He called out to her again, but still nothing.

He pulled away some of the fallen boulders. All the tugging and pulling didn't seem to be getting him anywhere. He needed help.

He raced to his SUV, drove like a bat out of hell to the entrance of the canyon. He checked his phone.

Thankfully every bar was lit up.

He called dispatch, advised them of the situation. He closed the phone and tucked it into his jacket pocket.

A patrol car was already en route based

on Bree's sister's frantic call. Dispatch would notify search and rescue. They would be here soon.

But would it be soon enough?

Bree stirred.

Was that a scraping sound?

She listened.

Maybe she'd imagined it.

Peter had finally fallen asleep. She touched his forehead. Checked to see that he was breathing steadily.

She shook the flashlight when it tried to go dim.

If Patrick was hurt…

He could be lying out there, dying.

No. She refused to believe that. He would find a way to overtake the shooter and then he would bring help.

She was sure of it.

Her head ached. She reached up and rubbed at her forehead. Something damp and sticky stuck to her fingers.

She looked at her fingers in the light.

Blood.

She shuddered. She was bleeding.

As if she'd only just then become aware of her own injuries, her body ached. Her back. Her right arm. And her head. Her head throbbed like hell.

But she was okay.

More importantly Peter's injury didn't appear to be life-threatening.

Bree reflected on the stories she'd told her son before he'd drifted to sleep. With each one the memories of how very much she had loved Patrick stacked one on top of the other.

She'd been young and impulsive and too career focused. She'd walked away from a relationship that could have been the forever kind.

Worse, she had deprived her son of a complete family unit.

If she made it out of here she would ensure her son knew his father. She couldn't change the past but she could make it right from here on out.

That scraping sound grated against her eardrums again.

Hope bloomed in her chest.

Had Patrick brought help?

She eased carefully away from Peter and scrambled toward where the opening had collapsed.

Putting her head against the pile of rubble, she listened intently.

Voices. More scraping.

Yes! He had brought help.

Her first thought was to wake Peter and tell him but she should let him sleep. As long as he was asleep he wouldn't be suffering from pain.

She wanted to shout Patrick's name but that would awaken Peter.

So she waited. Waited and listened.

The rocks piled between her and freedom suddenly shifted, started to fall this way and that.

She clambered out of the way.

A ray of sunlight pierced the darkness. She held her hand in front of her face and blinked to adjust to the new brightness.

"Bree!"

Patrick.

"Yes! We're here!"

Her heart thumped harder and harder. They were going to be okay. And Patrick was alive.

She repeated a silent mantra thanking God for protecting them.

When enough of the rubble was out of the way so that she could see Patrick's face among the others working to free her, she wept.

She scrambled over to where Peter lay and gently roused him.

He moaned and agony speared her heart.

"Baby, they're here to help us."

Peter's eyes fluttered open. "My daddy?"

Bree's lips trembled into a smile. "Yes, your daddy and his friends are here to take us out of this place."

Peter licked his lips. "My leg hurts."

"I know, sweetie. We'll make it all better soon."

Everything started to happen at once then. A paramedic came through the opening first.

"What've we got, Detective?"

"I'm okay," she insisted, despite the way the paramedic was looking at her head with his heavy-duty light. "But my son's left leg appears to be broken. The calf area."

The paramedic moved next to Peter. "Hey, little man, let me have a look at you."

Suddenly Patrick was next to her. He hugged her so tight she couldn't breathe. Bree cried against his strong shoulder.

"Thank you," she murmured.

"Mommy!"

Bree pulled away from Patrick and went to her son. The paramedic gave him something for the pain before attempting to move him.

The portable gurney came in next and slowly but surely Peter was transferred onto it. Once the gurney was through the opening, Patrick helped Bree climb out.

Patrick looked at her in the light. "You're hurt."

"It doesn't matter." She looked around. "What about the shooter?"

"It was your ex," Patrick explained,

pulling her against his chest. "But I took care of him. They've taken him away already. He was in need of a few stitches."

Bree tried to smile. It hurt. She was glad Jack the Bully had finally gotten his due. A part of her couldn't believe he'd gone so far as to try and kill her and Peter, but the cop in her wasn't really surprised. Violent men like him often escalated. "I should have seen this coming." She shook her head. Puffed out the frustration that tried to build. The cold, hard fact that the bastard could have killed her baby suddenly shook her hard. And she hadn't even seen it coming.

"Don't go there, Bree," Patrick warned. "You couldn't have known he was capable of this." His arm went around her waist. "Now come on. You need medical attention."

Before she could assure him that she was okay, he'd shouted for a paramedic.

The next thing she knew she was in an ambulance with Peter. He lay still on the gurney but his breathing was slow and steady. The drugs had kicked in.

"I'll be waiting at the hospital," Patrick promised before the paramedic closed the door.

Bree held on to that promise the entire trip. The paramedic cleaned up her head wound. Nothing a little tape couldn't take care of. She probably had a ton of bruises. But she would live. She and her son were safe.

Patrick was safe.

That was all she could ask for.

Chapter Twelve

Patrick paced the corridor outside the treatment room. An orthopedist had been called in to properly set and immobilize Peter's leg.

Patrick closed his eyes and thanked God once more. Bree was a little banged up but it was nothing serious. And Peter would be fine.

Jack Raintree was in jail where he belonged.

Patrick's mother was in the lobby. As were Bree's sister and niece, Callie MacBride, Tom Ryan and Steve Cyrus.

Ryan had let Patrick know that Watts had been released. They had nothing to hold him beyond the drunk and disorderly Kenner City PD had charged him with.

Watts wasn't confessing and the hearsay his drunken friend had passed along wasn't enough. But, Ryan had assured him, Watts was on their watch list.

The door to the treatment room opened and Patrick whirled in that direction.

"He's ready to go home," Doctor Ellis announced.

"Thanks, Doc."

As soon as the doctor had cleared the doorway, Patrick strode into the room.

Bree and a nurse were helping Peter into a wheelchair.

"I'll pull my vehicle into the pickup area," Patrick offered since there didn't appear to be anything else he could do.

"That would be nice." Bree looked totally spent.

"I'll meet you in the lobby."

Patrick hustled out to the parking lot where he'd left his SUV. He rushed around to the pickup point outside the lobby doors. By the time he was back inside Peter was being wheeled into the lobby by the nurse. Bree walked alongside him.

Damn, she looked ready to drop.

Patrick's mother and Bree's family were treating Peter as if he were a prince. Hugs were exchanged between the women. Ryan, MacBride and Cyrus were letting Bree know how happy they were that she and Peter were all right.

Patrick felt a little like an outsider, but he pushed it away. He wasn't allowing his need to be front and center override what his heart was telling him.

Callie hugged Bree. As did Cyrus. Ryan clapped her on the back.

"Let's get this young man headed home," the nurse suggested.

It was hospital policy that all patients left via wheelchair and accompanied by a nurse.

"I'll stay with you tonight," Tabitha offered to Bree.

"You and Layla go home," Bree insisted. "We'll be fine. We'll need you enough the next few weeks as it is."

Tabitha resisted a bit, but then gave in. Goodbyes were exchanged as the entourage following the wheelchair moved toward the door.

Before going through the automatic doors, Patrick glanced back at those who'd come to see that Peter and Bree were safe.

Callie MacBride lingered behind. She had her cell phone in hand. She stared at the screen a moment, then stepped farther away from the others before taking the call.

Judging by the look on her face the caller had relayed some earth-shattering news. She listened for a few moments, made a brief comment and shut her phone. Hard. She shoved it back into her purse.

Between Callie and Parrish, they had the monopoly on strange behavior.

Patrick helped his son into his SUV and drove him and Bree home. The ride was silent. Everyone was too tired to talk.

When they parked in Bree's drive, she opened the passenger-side door. "I'll get the front door."

Patrick carried Peter to the house. He couldn't begin to describe the amazing feeling of holding his son in his arms.

When Peter had been deposited into his bed and tucked in for the night, Patrick followed Bree to the kitchen. He felt a little like an obedient dog waiting for his next order. There was so much he wanted to say but he didn't know where to begin.

He was just so damned thankful that Bree and Peter were going to be fine.

But he couldn't keep standing here. He had to say something.

"So, how are we going to handle this?" He knew she was exhausted, but he needed some kind of reassurance.

Whatever it took, he would make their relationship work. Even if it turned out to only be one based on friendship.

Bree leaned against the counter. "I talked to Peter a lot while we were trapped. He wants to get to know you and spend time with you." She managed a halfhearted laugh. "Watch out or he'll be taking you to school for show and tell."

Patrick reached up and pushed her dark hair away from her taped wound. "And you and me, what do we do about that?"

"We take it one day at a time."

Patrick could handle that. "Sounds reasonable."

"But we'll still be a family." She exhaled a weary breath. "We'll do things together, share holidays. Just like any normal family."

"With you working in homicide and me the sheriff of Kenner County, I'm not sure we'll ever be normal."

Bree smiled dimly. "Maybe not, but we'll figure it out as we go."

"You should go to bed."

Bree looked in the direction of the hall leading to the bedrooms. "I don't know. I'm so exhausted. I'm afraid once I fall asleep I won't hear him if he needs me."

"I'll stay." Patrick took her by the elbow and started guiding her toward the hall. Her room had to be one of the two on either side of Peter's. "If he needs anything I'll take care of it."

"Tabitha or Layla could come over."

"Nope. I'm staying. No arguments."

Bree pointed to the bedroom just beyond Peter's. "That's mine."

Patrick ushered her through the door and onto the bed. He tugged off her shoes and spread a blanket over her. "I'll crash on the couch. If you need anything, just give a holler."

When he would have turned away, Bree said, "Patrick?"

He looked back at her. His heart squeezed at how vulnerable she looked. And at the same time she was the most beautiful woman he had ever seen. Her long dark hair was loose from its braid. He yearned to touch it…to touch her.

She patted the bed beside her. "Lay with me."

When he hesitated, she said, "Please. I just want you near me."

Lying next to her without touching her would be one of the hardest things he'd ever done, but he wouldn't deny her that comfort for anything in the world.

He settled on the bed next to her. Took her hand in his.

Just lying there staring at her profile and holding her hand was suddenly enough.

She turned to him. "I've always loved you, Patrick. Somehow it got all tangled up in other things, but it never went away. I'm sorry… I was wrong." She closed her eyes. "So wrong."

"Shh." He touched her lips. "We've both made mistakes. Grown up a lot. We start from here." He smiled. "And it's a good thing you still love me. 'Cause I never stopped loving you."

She reached up, touched his face. Her cool fingertips traced his jaw. "You're right. We are older. We'll take it slow. Do it right this time."

"We'll do it right," he agreed. He kissed her nose. "Sleep. You need the rest. I'll be here when you wake up."

Bree closed her eyes and he watched her drift into slumber.

She didn't ever have to worry again. He would always be here for her…and for his son.

Epilogue

Two weeks later...

Bree walked through the gift shop. Today was Peter's first day back at school since his injury. She wanted to get him a special gift to celebrate how brave he'd been through this entire ordeal.

She couldn't get over how quickly he and Patrick had bonded. It was like they'd always been together.

It made her heart glad.

Her cell phone vibrated. She glanced at the screen. Her lips stretched into a smile. Speak of the devil.

She opened the phone. "What's up, Sheriff?"

"I was thinking you might be available for lunch."

"Definitely. In fact I took the afternoon off."

"What a coincidence. So did I."

Desire swam through her veins. She and Patrick had progressed to long kissing sessions. Making out, as he called it. She was ready for the next step.

"I think I might have just enough time to have a leisurely lunch before it's time to pick up Peter."

"Meet me at my place in half an hour."

"Are you cooking?" Anticipation lit inside her.

"Definitely."

"Half an hour," she promised.

Bree tucked her phone away and moved a little more quickly through the shop. The prospect of finally making love with Patrick again after all these years had her on fire.

She passed a long row of jewelry made by Ute craftsmen. One of the necklaces snagged her attention. She backed up and took a second look.

Her heart bumped against her sternum.

Almost in slow motion, she reached out and touched the chain. Picked it up and examined it more closely. She'd seen it before. It was so familiar.

Everything inside her stilled.

"Oh, my God." The pattern of the silver chain was exactly the same.

A perfect match to the ligature pattern on Julie Grainger's throat.

This, or a chain like this, was the murder weapon.

* * * * *

KENNER COUNTY CRIME UNIT
continues next month with
PROFILE DURANGO by Carla Cassidy.
Don't miss any of this fast-paced action,
only from Harlequin Intrigue.

*Celebrate 60 years of pure reading
pleasure with Harlequin® Books!*

*Harlequin Romance® is celebrating by
showering you with DIAMOND
BRIDES in February 2009.
Six stories that promise to bring a touch
of sparkle to your life, with diamond
proposals and dazzling weddings,
sparkling brides and gorgeous grooms!*

*Enjoy a sneak peek at
Caroline Anderson's
TWO LITTLE MIRACLES,
available February 2009
from Harlequin Romance®.*

"I'VE FOUND HER."

Max froze.

It was what he'd been waiting for since June, but now—now he was almost afraid to voice the question. His heart stalling, he leaned slowly back in his chair and scoured the investigator's face for clues. "Where?" he asked, and his voice sounded rough and unused, like a rusty hinge.

"In Suffolk. She's living in a cottage."

Living. His heart crashed back to life, and he sucked in a long, slow breath. All these months he'd feared—

"Is she well?"

"Yes, she's well."

He had to force himself to ask the next question. "Alone?"

The man paused. "No. The cottage belongs to a man called John Blake. He's working away at the moment, but he comes and goes."

God. He felt sick. So sick he hardly registered the next few words, but then gradually they sank in. "She's got *what*?"

"Babies. Twin girls. They're eight months old."

"Eight—?" he echoed under his breath. "They must be his."

He was thinking out loud, but the P.I. heard and corrected him.

"Apparently not. I gather they're hers. She's been there since mid-January last year, and they were born during the summer—June, the woman in the post office thought. She was more than helpful. I think there's been a certain amount of speculation about their relationship."

He'd just bet there had. God, he was going to kill her. Or Blake. Maybe both of them.

"Of course, looking at the dates, she was

presumably pregnant when she left you, so they could be yours, or she could have been having an affair with this Blake character before…"

He glared at the unfortunate P.I. "Just stick to your job. I can do the math," he snapped, swallowing the unpalatable possibility that she'd been unfaithful to him before she'd left. "Where is she? I want the address."

"It's all in here," the man said, sliding a large envelope across the desk to him. "With my invoice."

"I'll get it seen to. Thank you."

"If there's anything else you need, Mr. Gallagher, any further information—"

"I'll be in touch."

"The woman in the post office told me Blake was away at the moment, if that helps," he added quietly, and opened the door.

Max stared down at the envelope, hardly daring to open it, but when the door clicked softly shut behind the P.I., he eased up the flap, tipped it and felt his breath jam in his throat as the photos spilled out over the desk.

Oh, Lord, she looked gorgeous. Different, though. It took him a moment to recognize her, because she'd grown her hair, and it was tied back in a ponytail, making her look younger and somehow freer. The blond highlights were gone, and it was back to its natural soft golden-brown, with a little curl in the end of the ponytail that he wanted to thread his finger through and tug, just gently, to draw her back to him.

Crazy. She'd put on a little weight, but it suited her. She looked well and happy and beautiful, but oddly, considering how desperate he'd been for news of her for the past year—one year, three weeks and two days, to be exact—it wasn't only Julia who held his attention after the initial shock. It was the babies sitting side by side in a supermarket trolley. Two identical and absolutely beautiful little girls.

* * .* * *

When Max Gallagher hires a P.I. to find his estranged wife, Julia, he discovers she's not alone—she has twin baby girls, and they might be his. Now workaholic Max has just two weeks to prove that he can be a wonderful husband and father to the family he wants to treasure.

Look for TWO LITTLE MIRACLES
by Caroline Anderson,
available February 2009
from Harlequin Romance®.

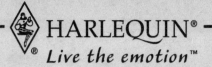

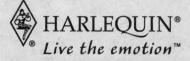

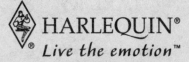

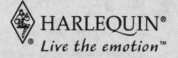

HARLEQUIN®
Presents®

**The world's bestselling romance series...
The series that brings you your favorite authors,
month after month:**

Helen Bianchin...Emma Darcy
Lynne Graham...Penny Jordan
Miranda Lee...Sandra Marton
Anne Mather...Carole Mortimer
Melanie Milburne...Michelle Reid

and many more talented authors!

Wealthy, powerful, gorgeous men...
Women who have feelings just like your own...
The stories you love, set in exotic, glamorous locations...

HARLEQUIN®
Presents®

Seduction and Passion Guaranteed!

HPDIR08